And that was what scared him.

As he softened the kiss, then slowly withdrew, his gaze met her blue eyes, glazed with passion…and he was tempted to drag her into his arms again.

Fighting the desire to do something he'd regret, Hank stepped back and forced a teasing grin to his mouth. "See?" he said. "That wasn't so bad, was it?"

Bad? It was anything but bad, Leighanna thought numbly, her blood still racing like fire through her veins. But Hank's casual remark infuriated her, and his indifferent stance made him vulnerable to the force of the hand that suddenly streaked out and slapped the side of his face.

"What was that for?" he asked incredulously.

"I warned you once," Leighanna said, fighting to keep the tremble from her voice. "Next time, you better think twice before kissing me."

Dear Reader,

This month we have some special treats in store for you, beginning with *Nobody's Princess,* another terrific MAN OF THE MONTH from award-winning writer Jennifer Greene. Our heroine believes she's just another run-of-the-mill kind of gal…but naturally our hero knows better. And he sets out to prove to her that he is her handsome prince…and she is his princess!

Joan Elliott Pickart's irresistible Bishop brothers are back in *Texas Glory,* the next installment of her FAMILY MEN series. And Amy Fetzer brings us her first contemporary romance, a romantic romp concerning parenthood—with a twist—in *Anybody's Dad.* Peggy Moreland's heroes are always something special, as you'll see in *A Little Texas Two-Step,* the latest in her TROUBLE IN TEXAS series.

And if you're looking for fun and frolic—and a high dose of sensuality—don't miss Patty Salier's latest, *The Honeymoon House.* If emotional and dramatic is more your cup of tea, then you'll love Kelly Jamison's *Unexpected Father.*

As always, there is something for everyone here at Silhouette Desire, where you'll find the very best contemporary romance.

Enjoy!

Lucia Macro

Senior Editor

Please address questions and book requests to:
Silhouette Reader Service
U.S.: 3010 Walden Ave., P.O. Box 1325, Buffalo, NY 14269
Canadian: P.O. Box 609, Fort Erie, Ont. L2A 5X3

PEGGY MORELAND
A LITTLE TEXAS TWO-STEP

SILHOUETTE *Desire*®
Published by Silhouette Books
America's Publisher of Contemporary Romance

To Jean Brashear, the quintessential friend.
And a special thanks to Snuffy's of Hutto, Texas, for inspiration in creating The End of the Road bar!

 SILHOUETTE BOOKS

ISBN 0-373-76090-6

A LITTLE TEXAS TWO-STEP

Copyright © 1997 by Peggy Bozeman Morse

This edition published by arrangement with Harlequin Books S.A.

® and TM are trademarks of Harlequin Books S.A., used under license. Trademarks indicated with ® are registered in the United States Patent and Trademark Office, the Canadian Trade Marks Office and in other countries.

Printed in U.S.A.

Books by Peggy Moreland

Silhouette Desire

A Little Bit Country #515
Run for the Roses #598
Miss Prim #682
The Rescuer #765
Seven Year Itch #837
The Baby Doctor #867
Miss Lizzy's Legacy #921
A Willful Marriage #1024
*Marry Me, Cowboy #1084
*A Little Texas Two-Step #1090

Silhouette Special Edition

Rugrats and Rawhide #1084

*Trouble in Texas

PEGGY MORELAND

published her first romance with Silhouette in 1989. She's a natural storyteller with a sense of humor that will tickle your fancy, and Peggy's goal is to write a story that readers will remember long after the last page is turned. Winner of the 1992 National Readers' Choice Award and a 1994 RITA finalist, Peggy frequently appears on bestseller lists around the country. A native Texan, she and her family live in Round Rock, Texas.

Dear Reader,

Women. Man, I love 'em! The shape of 'em, the feel of 'em, the scent of 'em. Nothing compares to rolling around on a bed with a willing woman, taking a little pleasure and giving a ton of it in return, sleeping all cuddled up next to a soft and curvy body, then waking up the next morning revitalized and ready for another tangle on the sheets. Man, that's what I call life!

Variety. I like that, too, which is why I'm a confirmed bachelor. I always let a woman know up front that I'm not interested in a permanent relationship, but occasionally one will start making those little possessive noises, and that's when I start backpedaling. I'm not interested in marriage. No, sirree, not me! I like my life just the way it is…or at least I did until Leighanna came along.

Leighanna. The epitome of woman. Soft. Feminine. Sexy. Passionate. But with a streak of stubbornness in her that defies a man's patience. She happened along, looking for a job, and against my better judgment I hired her on as a waitress at The End of the Road. My life hasn't been the same since.

Misery. That's what life is like without Leighanna. Have you ever felt like there's this hole where your heart used to be? I don't know how it happened, or even when, but that's exactly how I feel whenever Leighanna isn't around. Do you think this is love? The forever kind? Nah, it couldn't be. Could it…?

Hank Braden

Prologue

The minute she opened the door of her apartment, Leigh-anna smelled him. Polo. That spicy, sexy scent that her ex couldn't afford but always somehow managed to find the money to purchase.

She stopped, her key cutting into the palm of one hand, her suitcase cinched tight in the other. He can't be here, she told herself in growing panic. He didn't have a key any longer, and there was no way in hell that Reggie, her friend and the owner of the apartment complex, would ever let him inside.

Yet the scent of him continued to taunt her.

Her legs trembled in fear, but she forced them into motion, taking one cautious step, then another, until she stood in the center of her small living room.

"Roger?" she called hesitantly. "Are you here?"

She waited a moment, listening, but only the muted click of her mantel clock as it ticked off each second disturbed the quiet. If he wasn't here, she knew he *had* been. The scent of his cologne still hung thick in the air. But how did he get in? she asked herself in growing dread. She'd changed the locks after she'd kicked him out more than a year before.

The handle of her suitcase slipped from her fingers, and she drew her shaking fingers to her lips. Her key ring! She'd given him her key ring over a month ago when he'd offered to take her car in for repairs.

Her fingers closed into a fist against her lips as she remembered the incident. Of course, he *hadn't* had her car repaired. Instead, he'd paid some shady mechanic a pittance of what she'd given him and instructed the man to do what he could without replacing the transmission, then pocketed the rest of the money for himself. Naturally, Roger hadn't told her about his clever little scheme. She'd discovered it on her own, weeks later, when the transmission had gone out on her in the middle of Houston's five-o'clock traffic.

She was sure that at the same time Roger had been having her car repaired, he'd probably had a duplicate set of keys made to every key on her ring...including the one to her apartment.

Anger burned through her. She knew better than to trust her ex-husband. Hadn't she learned anything during the four years of their marriage? He was the master of lies and deception. And she knew without a doubt that he wouldn't think twice about stealing from her. He'd done it often enough in the past. A twenty here, a hundred there, missing from her purse. After their divorce, he'd even taken her wedding ring from her jewelry box and pawned it, spending the money on some new scam.

Money! Her fingers curled around the key ring as a new fear rose. With her heart thundering against her chest, she ran to the kitchen and jerked a canister from those that lined the counter beside the sink...and listened to the sick clink of loose coins. She knew even before she opened it that it was gone. All that she'd managed to save toward the purchase of a new car. She tipped the canister upside down, and pennies rained onto the floor.

Tears swelled and the canister blurred before her eyes. Raising the container above her head, she screamed, "Damn you, Roger!" and hurled it against the far wall where it shattered into a hundred jagged pieces right along with her dreams for a new car.

Reggie Giles frowned at the open apartment door then stepped inside, knocking on the door as she passed. "Leighanna?" she called as she stopped in the living room. "Leighanna, where are you?"

"I'm back here," came Leighanna's muffled reply. "In my room."

Anxious to hear about Leighanna's visit with their friend Mary Claire in her new home in Temptation, Reggie headed down the short hall.

"Did you know you left your front door open?" she scolded. "Anybody could come in and—"

At the door to Leighanna's bedroom, Reggie stopped cold. A suitcase lay on the bed, a tangle of clothes and shoes tumbled over its side, wire hangers were scattered over the floor. Leighanna stood in front of the dresser, jerking handfuls of lingerie and socks from the drawers.

Reggie let out a slow, long breath, unsure of what was happening. "Are you coming or going?" she asked uneasily.

Leighanna whirled. Her eyes were red, her cheeks mottled by anger. "Going!" She marched past Reggie and dumped the load she carried into the suitcase.

"Where?" Reggie asked.

"I'm moving out."

Fear knotted in Reggie's stomach. Leighanna was like family to her, as was Mary Claire, and she'd already lost Mary Claire and her children when they'd moved to Temptation. She couldn't bear the thought of losing Leighanna, too.

When Leighanna brushed past her again, headed for the dresser, Reggie grabbed her arm. "Wait a second," she said, hoping to slow Leighanna down long enough to find out what was behind this quick exodus. "Why are you moving out?"

Leighanna jerked free of Reggie's hold. "Roger!" she snapped, and marched on to the dresser. She snatched an armful of clothing from the bottom drawer, then kicked it closed with her foot.

Reggie could only stare. She had never seen Leighanna like this before. Always calm, soft-spoken, Leighanna seldom lost her temper. She was generous and loving and giving...even to that scumball of an ex-husband of hers, Roger.

And that's exactly what he was, too, Reggie thought angrily. Leighanna might have been blinded to his faults, but Reggie had never been. She had leased Roger the apartment four years ago when he'd first married Leighanna and would have kicked the loser out years ago when his first rent check had bounced if she hadn't felt sorry for his poor wife. She'd held Leighanna's hand throughout the divorce, had even tried to open Leighanna's eyes to his scheming ways when he would drop by periodically after their divorce, trying to borrow money from her. But Leighanna was naive and totally trusting, and never saw through his deceit until it was too late.

That he was behind this fit of temper didn't surprise

her. What worried her was what Roger had done to pro-
voke it.

"What does he have to do with your moving out?"
she asked uneasily.

Leighanna turned on Reggie, her hands filled with
clothes, her blue eyes wild with anger. "You'd think it
would be enough for him that he ruined my life right
along with my credit, wouldn't you?" she raged. "But,
no! Not Roger! He's like that damn bunny in the battery
commercial, pounding his drum. He just keeps going and
going and going!"

Reggie sank to the edge of the bed, her shoulders
slumping. "What has he done now?" she asked in res-
ignation.

Leighanna threw the armload of clothes into the suitcase and planted her hands on her hips as she whirled to
face Reggie. "He came into my apartment while I was
gone to visit Mary Claire and stole all my money from
the cookie jar."

Reggie was on her feet in a flash. "He did what?" she
cried.

"He stole my money! All that I had saved to buy a
new car."

Angry now herself, Reggie paced away, fisting her
hands at her sides. "Well, he won't get away with it this
time. Not if I have any say in the matter." Always ready
to take charge, Reggie mentally listed what would need
to be done. "We're calling the police. We'll file charges
for breaking and entering and for burglary. When they
find him, they'll throw his lousy butt in jail, and this time
we'll see that they throw away the key." She stopped
and wheeled, thrusting a warning finger at Leighanna.
"Don't touch another thing," she ordered. "The police
will need to dust the apartment for prints."

Leighanna went right on throwing clothes into the suitcase. "Forget it, Reggie. The police can't do anything."

"And why not?" she asked incredulously. "He broke into your apartment and stole your money. Last I remember, that's still a crime."

"He didn't break in. He used a key."

"A key!" Reggie all but screamed. "For God's sake, Leighanna, you gave him a key?"

"No, I didn't *give* him a key." The fight suddenly went out of Leighanna and she dropped down on the edge of the bed and covered her face with her hands. "He must have had a duplicate made last month when he took my car to have it repaired."

"Repaired?" Reggie repeated sarcastically. "You mean when he fleeced you of the repair money, don't you?" She dropped down on the bed beside Leighanna in frustration. "Geez, Leighanna! When will you ever learn? The man can't be trusted."

Leighanna dragged her hands down her face then tipped her face to the ceiling. "I know. I know," she said miserably. "But he said he knew somebody who could replace the transmission cheaper, and that he wanted to do it for me to make up for all the money he owed me."

Reggie just rolled her eyes. It would be just like Leighanna to fall for a line like that. "Well, there's still the burglary charge," Reggie reminded her. "We can nail him with that."

Leighanna turned to look at Reggie, her expression one of defeat. "And you think the police will believe me? I can't prove that the money was there and I certainly can't prove that Roger took it." She pushed to her feet and straightened. "Forget it, Reggie. There's only one thing left for me to do and that is to move."

Reggie jumped from the bed. "And what will you solve by moving?"

"I'll be away from him. Far away. Somewhere where he'll never think to look for me."

"And where would that be?"

"Temptation. I'm moving in with Mary Claire and her kids."

One

Hank caught a movement out of the corner of his eye and glanced toward the entrance to his bar. A woman stood before the front window, bent at the waist, her chin thrust forward as she peered through its dirty glass.

Hank muttered a curse. He was sick and damn tired of people sticking their noses in his window at all hours of the day. The sign on the door clearly read Closed, but that little fact didn't seem to bother the throng of people who'd made their way to Temptation.

And it's all Cody's fault, he grumped silently, thinking of his friend and Temptation's sheriff. If he hadn't come up with the fool notion to advertise for women to save Temptation from becoming a ghost town, all these folks wouldn't have converged on their town.

He watched, frowning, as the sun panned gold from the woman's shoulder-length blond hair while the wind whipped it across her face. She caught the long tresses that curtained one cheek in long, delicately boned fingers to hold it back from her face.

Scrawny little thing, he told himself as he watched her. Probably didn't weigh more than a hundred pounds dripping wet. He stepped around the bar to get a better look. Yep, he confirmed, she was scrawny all right. Her arms were thin as reeds, her shoulders narrow, and if she had any boobs at all beneath that baggy silk blouse, she was hiding them well.

Hank snorted and shook his head. Personally, he liked his women with a little more flesh on them. Full hips made for a man to ride, breasts big enough to fill his hands, lips thick enough to wrap around his—

At that moment, she glanced up and caught sight of him through the window and offered him a tentative smile.

Well, she had the lips, he admitted reluctantly. And the pearliest white teeth he'd ever seen. While he watched, she snagged the sign from the window he'd put there three days before. She disappeared for a moment, only to reappear on the other side of the locked front door. She tapped on the glass then pointed to the sign she held.

Hank groaned. "Damn," he muttered under his breath, knowing full well that she was wanting to apply for the waitress position he'd advertised for. And Hank knew damn good and well this was going to be a waste of his time. She couldn't handle the job. The work was backbreaking, the hours long, his customers rowdy at best. A slip of a woman like her wouldn't last one shift as a waitress in a bar like The End of the Road.

Muttering curses under his breath, he crossed to the door and unlocked it. "Can I help you?"

Leighanna took a step back and pressed the sign to her

breasts, startled by the intimidating size and the gruffness of the man who stood opposite her. Tall, broad-shouldered, slim-hipped, he had the face of an angel but the eyes and the mouth of the devil himself. ''I hope so,'' she said, then nervously wet her lips.

The dart of that pink tongue made Hank think of other things he'd like that tongue to do. Before he had time to follow that train of thought, though, she extended her hand.

''I'm Leighanna Farrow,'' she said by way of intro-duction. ''Are you the owner?''

Hank scowled. ''Yeah, I'm the owner.'' Reluctantly, he took her hand in his. ''Hank Braden.''

Her hand was smooth as silk against his callused palm and soft as butter, further proof that she wasn't fit for the job.

She pushed a smile to her lips as she withdrew her hand...but he could see the fear in her eyes, could almost smell it over the scent of her perfume. His customers would eat a woman like her alive.

''I'd like to apply for the waitress position,'' she said politely, and offered him the sign.

Hank took it and stuck it right back in the window. ''Sorry. You're not what I had in mind.''

Her mouth dropped open. ''But—''

''Lady,'' he growled. ''This is a bar, not some damn tearoom. You wouldn't last five minutes in a place like this.''

Her chin came up, her blue eyes as sharp as tempered steel. ''And how would you know?''

Hank snorted, then took his gaze on a slow journey from the top of her blond head to the tips of her high-heeled mules. She looked like one of those damn Dream-sicle ice cream bars, standing there in those peach-colored leggings and that baggy, watered silk blouse, looking all soft and creamy and temptingly sweet. And though he was tempted to offer her something other than a job, he knew sampling her would only bring him grief. By the regal lift of her chin and the cut of the clothes she wore, he figured she was a little classy for his taste, as well as that of his bar.

A sardonic smile tipped one corner of his mouth as his eyes met hers again. "Trust me," he said. "I just know." He turned his back on her and walked away.

Leighanna watched him and felt her last chance for employment slipping from her fingers. She needed this job, she told herself. She'd already walked the main street of Temptation, seeking employment in every possible establishment, but there wasn't a job to be had...other than this one.

Squaring her shoulders in determination, she yanked the sign from the window and hurried to catch up with him, her mules slapping against her heels and clicking loudly against the scarred linoleum floor. "Mr. Braden—"

Hank wheeled and she skidded to a stop to keep from bumping into the wall of his chest. The woman was as pesky as a fly that just wouldn't shoo. "The name's Hank," he snapped. "And I said no."

If his size wasn't enough to send her running for her car, the threatening look in his eye should have done the trick. But it didn't. Leighanna was that desperate. Her creditors were already breathing down her neck. "Hank, then," she said, and fought to hide the tremble in her lips. "Look. I really need this job."

Hank heaved a sigh, then folded his arms across his chest. "Have you ever worked as a waitress before?"

"No," she replied reluctantly.

"Well, what makes you think you can do the work?"

"I managed a clothing boutique in Houston before I moved here, so I'm accustomed to dealing with the public. And I'm a fast learner," she was quick to add. "Plus, I'm willing to do whatever work is required."

He curled his mouth in disgust. "You don't even know what the job entails."

"No," she agreed in a voice as soft as her skin. "But perhaps you could enlighten me."

Deciding the best way to get rid of her might be to tell her exactly what he expected of her, Hank grabbed a chair from the top of the table and plopped it onto the floor. He hiked a boot on the seat of the chair, folded his arms across his knee and narrowed an eye at her. "In the past, I've worked the place by myself, but with all these damn strangers that keep pouring into town as a result of the media attention Temptation's received, business has picked up and I need help.

"I work the bar and the grill myself, and I'd expect you to take the orders and deliver them. That means carrying trays loaded down with beer and food and clearing the tables when they're dirty. You'll do all the dishwashing, too. And you'll have to scrub out the toilets and mop the floors every night after we close."

He paused, measuring her response, but she didn't appear fazed one whit by what he'd described so far. He decided to shovel it on a little thicker.

"The men outnumber the women in this town about eight to one, and they're a rough lot. They spend most of their time alone on their ranches and farms and come in here on Friday and Saturday nights to blow off a little steam and have a good time. They'll probably find a woman like you hard to resist. But I expect you to keep your mind on your job and your skirt on...at least while you're on duty," he added with a wink.

Though she paled a little, she didn't turn tail and run as Hank had expected. He heaved a deep breath, wondering what it was going to take to get rid of her. "After they have a few drinks, the boys tend to get a little testy. If a fight breaks out, it's your job to bust it up." Her eyes widened a little and Hank decided he'd finally hit on the right vein. "When they're drunk enough to fight, they're usually drunk enough to puke. If they do, you'll be the one to clean it up."

Convinced by the sick look on her face that he'd painted the bleakest picture possible and there was no way in hell she'd want the waitressing job now, Hank dragged his boot from the chair. "Well, what do you think? You still interested?"

Leighanna swallowed hard. "How much does it pay?" she asked weakly.

"Minimum wage, but you can keep your tips...if you earn any," he added, sure that she would say thanks but no thanks.

He nearly keeled over when instead she said, "When do I start?"

"I found a job," Leighanna sang cheerfully as she stepped through the back door of Mary Claire's house.

Mary Claire turned from the sink. "You did?" she asked in surprise. A smile built when she saw the excited flush on Leighanna's cheeks. She quickly snatched up a cloth to dry her hands and hugged Leighanna to her. "That's wonderful!" she cried, then pushed Leighanna to arm's length. "Where?"

"The End of the Road."

Mary Claire's smile wilted as quickly as it had formed.

"The End of the Road? You mean that seedy little bar on the edge of town?"

Leighanna struggled to keep her smile in place. "Yes, that's the place. I start today at five." Ignoring Mary Claire's stricken expression, she ducked from beneath her arm and headed for the refrigerator. "Is there anything cold to drink? My car's air conditioner is still on the blink and it must be a hundred degrees outside."

"Yes," Mary Claire murmured, already wringing her hands. "I just made a pitcher of lemonade for the kids. Leighanna?" she asked nervously. "Are you sure you want to work in a place like that?"

"A place like what?" Leighanna asked innocently, though she knew full well what Mary Claire meant. The place was nothing but a glorified beer joint, but a job was a job, and beggars couldn't be choosers. Not in a town the size of Temptation.

Mary Claire forced her hands apart to pluck two glasses from the cupboard and trailed Leighanna to the table. "Well...I haven't been there myself, but I've heard that it gets pretty rough in there. Mrs. Martin over at the Mercantile told me that the sheriff is always having to go over there and break up fights on Saturday nights."

Leighanna silently cursed Hank Braden. Oh, he'd told her about the fights all right, but he hadn't said anything about the sheriff being the one to bust them up. She specifically remembered him saying that it would be up to *her* to settle any disputes. She wondered what else he had lied about.

Sighing, she filled the two glasses. It didn't matter whether he'd lied or not. She needed the money too much to complain. "It's the only job I could find," she said, and pushed a glass across the table before picking up her own.

Mary Claire shoved aside the offered drink and fisted her hands in a white-knuckled knot on the table. "If you need money that badly, I'll loan you some until something better comes along."

Leighanna shook her head. "You're already providing me room and board. I won't take your money."

Mary Claire heaved a sigh. "But, Leighanna—"

Leighanna leaned forward, covering Mary Claire's hand with hers, and squeezed, grateful to her friend for offering, but knowing she had to do this by herself.

When she'd left Houston, she'd been on the run, hoping to escape the power her ex-husband still held over her. But she knew that putting distance between herself and Roger wouldn't solve all her problems. She'd been a mouse where men were concerned, a doormat who had continually accepted whatever dirt the men in her life scraped her way in exchange for a little of their affection.

But not any longer. Leighanna was determined to change her ways. She'd already made a large step toward achieving this goal by standing up to Hank Braden and insisting that he give her the job. And though the thought of working for such a disagreeable man frightened her, she was determined to fend for herself, relying on no one and nothing other than her own abilities to pay her way.

"No, Mary Claire," she said firmly. "I won't take your money, though I do appreciate the offer."

When Leighanna arrived at five o'clock, Hank was already behind the bar, shoving long-neck beer bottles into an insulated box filled with ice. His hair was wet and slicked to one side, and though it was obvious he'd just shaved, his jaw still carried a five-o'clock shadow. "You're late," he grumped.

Leighanna glanced at her watch. "It's not even five," she said in surprise.

Hank jerked his head toward a clock behind the bar. The clock, like the rest of the bar's decor, had obviously been supplied by the beer distributor. A fake waterfall on the clock's face spilled over a mountain stream, and neon lights above it blinked on and off, advertising Coors beer.

The hands on the clock pointed to 5:03.

Leighanna knew darn good and well that her watch was accurate because she'd set it by the radio that very morning, but she also knew it wouldn't do any good to argue the point with Hank. Swallowing her retort, she quickly stored her purse on a shelf behind the bar. "I'm sorry. It won't happen again."

"It better not."

Though tempted to tell the man where he could shove his precious job, Leighanna bit her tongue and tied a towel around her waist. "What do you want me to do?" she asked.

Hank nodded toward the open room. "Take the chairs down and situate 'em around the tables, then check the salt and pepper shakers and make sure they're full. After you're done with that, you can chop lettuce and slice up enough tomatoes and onions to fill the bins there by the grill."

Sure that there was more to her job then the tasks he'd named, Leighanna frowned in puzzlement. "Is that all?"

"Nope," he said, and stopped long enough to shoot her a lazy grin. "But I know how you blondes are. I don't want to send your brain into overload by giving you too much to remember."

She knew he was baiting her, looking for any excuse to fire her before she ever started, and Leighanna refused to give him the pleasure. But that didn't stop the sweep of anger that burned her cheeks. Marching across the room, she started jerking chairs from the tops of the tables and shoving them up underneath.

Though Hank continued to stuff beer bottles into the cooler, he watched her out of the corner of his eye. Damn fool woman, he cursed silently. Didn't she know that silk didn't belong in a place like his? The slacks and matching blouse she wore looked as out of place in The End of the Road as she did. And those shoes she had on! Nothing but a handful of thin leather straps. Her feet would be killing her by closing time...if she lasted that long. As he watched, one of the baggy sleeves on her silk blouse caught on a splintered rung of the chair she was struggling to pull down. With a cry of dismay, she dropped the chair and it fell to the floor with a clatter as she lifted the sleeve to examine the snagged fabric. A soft, pitiful moan slipped from her lips.

Hank's blood heated in anger. He wouldn't feel sorry for her, he told himself. Any fool would know not to wear something like that to work as a waitress.

"Careful with the furniture," he snapped. "You break, you pay."

Her head came up, her chin jutting imperiously as her gaze met his and held. He saw the anger, the frustration in those blue depths, but ignored it. He'd tried to tell her she couldn't handle the job, but she wouldn't listen. So now she'd just have to learn it the hard way.

He waved a hand toward the tables. "Better get moving. You've still got those shakers to refill."

Leighanna dropped the sleeve with an indignant huff and stooped to turn the chair upright. Shoving it under the table with a little more force than necessary, she started snatching shakers from the centers of the tables. By the time she'd gathered them all, she'd calmed somewhat. She tried to lift the tray…and realized too late that she'd overloaded it.

She stole a glance at the bar and saw Hank watching her. She could tell by the measuring look in his eyes that this was all some kind of ridiculous test, and he was just waiting for her to fail. Determined to prove that she could handle the job, she set her jaw and lifted the tray. Straining under its weight, she staggered across the room, then had to hitch the tray's edge against her breasts for added leverage to raise it high enough to shove it onto the bar's high, scarred surface.

"Better be careful," Hank warned from the other side. "Or you'll smash what little bit God blessed you with."

Leighanna dropped the tray to the bar, her cheeks flaming, while salt and pepper shakers rolled crazily across its surface. Grabbing one before it toppled over the edge, she slammed it back down on the tray. "How much or how little God blessed me with is certainly no concern of yours," she said indignantly.

Hank arched a brow, his gaze dropping to her breasts. "No, but I've got eyes," he said, and grinned wickedly as he looked back up at her.

"Well, you can just keep your eyes to yourself," she snapped, and marched behind the bar. Not wanting to ask the aggravating man where he kept his supplies, she searched beneath the counter until she found the commercial-size containers of salt and pepper. Dragging them out to the bar, she started refilling the shakers.

Hank decided that this new waitress of his looked pretty cute when her feathers were all ruffled. Unable to resist ruffling them a little more, he eased up beside her, not close enough to touch, just close enough to let her know he was there. He heard her huff of breath and bit back a grin as he picked up a salt shaker and slowly unscrewed its top.

"No need to get your panties in a twist," he said mildly. "Some men like women with small breasts...I just don't happen to be one of them."

"Thank heaven for that," she muttered under her breath.

Acting as if he hadn't heard her, he poured salt into the shaker. "But some of the men who'll be coming in tonight aren't as selective as me. You might consider buttoning that blouse of yours up a little higher. You wouldn't want them to think you're advertising...unless you are, of course."

Frowning, Leighanna dipped her chin to look down at her blouse. Her eyes flew wide when she saw that the tray had pulled one of the buttons from its hole, exposing a generous view of a lace covered breast, a view she knew Hank had already taken advantage of. Quickly she grabbed the plackets together and forced the button back into place. "Thank you," she murmured in embarrassment, unable to look Hank in the eye.

Hank just chuckled and screwed the lid back on the shaker. "Don't mention it."

Leighanna was sure that he was doing it purposefully, just to fluster her, because everywhere she turned he was there, in her way, all but breathing down her neck.

"Don't you have anything to do?" she finally asked in frustration as she pushed a knife through a plump, red tomato.

He just grinned. "Am I bothering you?"

Juice dripped from her fingers as she tossed the thinly sliced tomato into the bin...and their shoulders bumped...again. "Yes," she said, and dug her shoulder into his and gave him an impatient shove.

"What am I doing that's bothering you?"

"You're—you're—"

"What?" he prodded.

Fighting for patience, she rested her wrists on the cutting board and turned, angling her body just enough to frown at him. But looking at him was a mistake. His eyes were filled with mischief, and his mouth was quirked in that teasing grin he'd worn ever since he'd warned her about her blouse.

Scowling, she twisted back around and grabbed an onion. "You're in my way," she muttered and slashed the knife through the onion, cutting it in half and sending its sharp aroma spiraling beneath her nose.

"Really?" he asked innocently and purposefully pressed his shoulder against hers again. "I don't mean to be. I'm just watching to make sure you know what you're doing."

The onion's odor was strong, burning her nose and filling her eyes with tears, but it was the heat from his body where their shoulders touched that she was most aware of. "I know what I'm doing," she replied, sniffing. "Any fool can slice vegetables." She lifted her hand to swipe a tear from her eye.

Hank caught her wrist in the width of one wide hand. Startled, she glanced up at him.

"I wouldn't do that if I were you," he warned. "You're liable to get onion juice in your eye, and it'll make it sting that much more." He caught up a towel. "Here, let me." He dabbed at the tears beneath her eyes, his touch gentle, his knuckles rough where they scraped against her cheek...and Leighanna wondered what he was up to. He'd already made it clear that he didn't want her in his bar, which made her suspicious of his kindness now.

He took his good easy time blotting her tears, then bent his knees and put his face level with hers. "How's that?"

She'd purposely avoided making eye contact with him all afternoon, but with him this close, she could do little else. The eyes that met hers were a dark brown, almost black, and his mouth less than a breath away. His features were almost too perfect, his forehead wide, his jaw square and shadowed, his cheekbones carved if by a sculptor's knife. His hair, thick and black, just brushed his collar and seemed to cry for a woman's hands. That he was aware of his sexual appeal was obvious in the cocky slant of his lips and the teasing glint in his eye.

Leighanna had known another man whose sex appeal equaled Hank's...and was still paying the price for falling prey to his charm. Determined not to fall again, she twisted back around and sniffed again. "Better, thank you."

Hank's grin broadened into a smile. "Good. I like to keep my employees satisfied."

"I'll just bet you do," she muttered under her breath.

Hank watched Leighanna from his spot behind the bar and grudgingly admitted that he might just have been wrong about her ability to handle this job. She sashayed between the tables, a tray propped on her open palm, smiling while she set mugs of beer in front of his customers. She made change, toted food, wiped up spills...and dodged the occasional straying hand.

He chuckled as he watched old Jack Barlow sneak an arm around her waist. Smooth as silk, she removed his hand, smiling sweetly enough not to offend the man before she headed back to the bar.

She shoved the empty tray onto the bar and sagged against it, mopping her damp brow with the back of her hand. At some point during the evening, she'd rolled her billowy sleeves to her elbows, revealing slender arms and even slimmer wrists. Her fingers were long and delicate and her almond-shaped nails were painted a light pink, almost the exact same shade as her blouse. A ketchup stain just above her right breast blotted the blouse's once perfect pink color.

"Two beers and a whiskey chaser," she said, raising her voice to be heard over the blaring jukebox.

Hank couldn't help but notice the weary slump of her shoulders. He stuck two frosted mugs under the tap. "Tired?" he asked.

Leighanna immediately straightened, not wanting to admit to her exhaustion. "No. Just hot."

Hank nodded sagely. "Yep. It's hot all right." He set the mugs on her tray and picked up a bottle of Jack Daniels. "You can take a break, if you want. I can keep an eye on things for a few minutes."

A break sounded wonderful after being on her feet for over six hours, but Leighanna quickly shook her head. She was determined not to give him any reason to doubt her abilities to handle the job. "No, I'm fine." She glanced at the clock behind the bar. "We'll be closing in less than an hour, anyway. I can wait until then."

Hank glanced at the clock, too, before adding the jigger of whiskey to the tray. "Your call, but remember we'll still have some work to do after they all clear out."

Leighanna stifled a groan, thinking of the toilets that would need scrubbing and the floor that would need mopping. She forced a perky smile. "Don't worry. I can handle it."

"Hey, Hank!" a man called from a corner of the room.

"Yo, what'cha need?" Hank called back.

"Has that little barrel racer from over Marble Falls way been back?"

Hank's chest swelled, and a gleam of what Leighanna could only describe as cockiness shown in his eyes.

"You mean Betty Jo?" Hank asked, trying hard not to smile as he curved his hands through the air, tracing a rather top-heavy hourglass shape.

The guy tossed back his head and laughed. "Yeah, that's the one."

"Nah, haven't seen her," Hank replied. "But she'll be back," he added, shooting the man a knowing wink. "They always do."

Leighanna snatched the tray from the bar and rolled her eyes as she turned away to deliver the drinks. "Men," she muttered under her breath.

Leighanna dropped the toilet brush into the bucket, then used her wrist to push her hair from her face. Lord, but she was tired. Her feet felt as if they were swollen twice their size, the leather bands of her sandals cutting viciously across her instep, and her calf muscles ached from all the walking...and she still had the floor to mop.

Groaning, she snagged the bucket's handle and limped from the bathroom and back out into the bar. Hank stood at the cash register, his lips moving silently as he slowly counted the night's proceeds. He glanced up, his gaze hitting hers and holding just long enough to make her want to squirm, before he nonchalantly went back to his counting.

The clock behind him read 12:45.

Stifling a moan, Leighanna trudged to the small kitchen and mixed up mop water, then hauled the bucket and mop back out front. With a scowl at Hank who hadn't done anything in the last half hour more strenuous than lift a handful of change from the cash drawer, she slapped the mop to the floor and began scrubbing. Back and forth, round and round, she swished the mop across the floor, the ache in her back growing until it was all she could do not to cry.

By the time she'd made her way back to the bar, the clock read 1:15. She'd put in over eight hours and it felt like eighteen. With no strength left in her arms, she dragged the bucket back to the kitchen and dumped the murky water down the drain.

Tugging the towel from her waist, she tossed it onto the bar, then ducked under it to retrieve her purse. "I'll be going now."

"Would you do me a favor before you leave?"

Already headed for the door, Leighanna stopped and wearily turned. "What?"

Hank gestured to the money stacked on the bar, then scratched his head. "I can't make the totals match. Would you mind recounting the money for me while I run the tickets again? It shouldn't take you more than a minute or two."

She doubted that, since he'd been counting the money the entire time she'd been scrubbing toilets and mopping floors. But it wouldn't hurt to prove to him that she could do more than scullery work. She tossed her purse onto the bar, climbed up onto a stool in front of it and grabbed a stack of bills. She quickly separated them into stacks of ones, fives, tens and twenties, then began to count, recording the totals of each stack on the back of an order blank.

Unaware that Hank had even moved, she suddenly realized that he had rounded the bar and stood beside her, his head tipped close to hers. She craned her neck to look at him. "What are you doing?" she asked, frowning.

He grinned. "Watching you."

"Well, don't!" she huffed impatiently, and snatched up another stack of bills.

"Why? Do I make you nervous?"

"Yes!" she said, and went back to her counting.

His nose bumped her neck and nuzzled. "You sure do smell nice."

She tried her best to ignore him, even managed to continue to slap down bills, silently counting, but heat raced through her as his nose traced the curve of her neck.

"What scent is that you're wearing?"

She dropped the money to the counter. "Do you want me to count this money, or not?" she asked in frustration.

"I think I'd rather you kissed me."

Her eyes widened and she jumped to her feet. "Kiss you!" she repeated, incensed that he would suggest such a thing.

"Yeah, you know. Press your lips against mine."

Leighanna snatched her purse from the counter and slung its strap across her shoulder. She stabbed a finger at his chest. "Let's get one thing straight, buster. You hired me to work as a waitress, not to service your more basic needs!"

Hank hooked his hands at his hips and whistled low through his teeth as he rocked back on the heels of his boots. "Man, oh man, but you sure are pretty when you're riled." Leaning forward, he crooked a finger and pressed its knuckle beneath her chin, forcing her face up to his. "But, honey, we need to get one more thing straight. Us kissing has absolutely nothing to do with you working for me. It's inevitable, that's all." He let his hand drop and shot her a wink. "But I'm a patient man."

* * *

Hank poked the key into the front door and turned it, glancing, as he did, out the window into the darkness beyond. Leighanna limped across the gravel parking lot, her shoulders stooped, as she headed for a shadowed car parked at the far end. He wanted to laugh at her sorry state, but couldn't quite work up the enthusiasm required for the task.

He supposed he should feel guilty for working her so hard, especially considering he'd shoved more than half his workload onto her slim shoulders...but he didn't. Hell, she was the one who'd wanted the job, he told himself, all but forcing him to hire her when he knew damn good and well she didn't have any business working in a place like The End of the Road.

His eyes went unerringly to the gentle sway of her hips. Even tired, the woman knew how to move. He blew out a slow breath. He didn't want to be attracted to her. Didn't even know why'd he'd bothered to tease her. He supposed it was just a natural reflex. Her being a woman, and all, and him being...well, him being just Hank.

A grin slowly built on his face. And Hank did love women. The feel of them, the taste of them, the feminine smell of them. Hell, he just liked women. And the fact that this one didn't seem interested in him only increased the challenge. For, as much as he liked women, Hank liked a challenge.

While he continued to watch, she opened the door to her car. The accompanying screech of metal made him wince. Squinting against the darkness, Hank looked at the car. It was a junker. Even from a distance, he could see that the windshield was cracked, the front bumper was missing, and the car's body had more rust than paint.

He heard the engine turn with a dragging *waaaa,*

waaa, waaa before it finally sparked to life, smoke pouring from the tailpipe at the rear. The headlights popped on, one a little brighter than the other, and he listened to the grinding of gears before the car finally chugged off.

What is a classy lady like her doing, driving a piece of crap like that? he wondered. Better yet, he asked himself, what was a classy lady like her doing in a two-bit town like Temptation?

Shaking his head, he pulled down the shade and headed for his room at the rear of the bar. Didn't matter why she was in Temptation, he told himself. She wouldn't be back at The End of the Road. Not after what he'd put her through tonight.

Two

"I swear, the man thinks he's God's gift to women!"

Mary Claire couldn't help but laugh as she set a pan of hot, steaming water on the stoop at Leighanna's feet. "From what I hear, he is."

Leighanna scowled, remembering the barrel racer mentioned the night before, and levered a heaping tablespoon of Epsom salts into the pan of hot water and stirred. She didn't want to ask, but couldn't resist. "What have you heard?"

Mary Claire sat down on the porch beside Leighanna and propped a bowl of peas on her lap. "Nothing specific, really. Just that he has quite a way with the women."

"He could have fooled me," Leighanna said dryly. She eased her swollen feet into the hot water and had to bite her lower lip to keep from crying.

Chuckling, Mary Claire patted her arm. "They'll feel

better after you've soaked them for a while." She picked up a pea pod and broke off its end. "Did you make much in tips last night?"

"A little over forty dollars."

"That's good, isn't it?"

"I suppose. But it doesn't come anywhere near matching the salary I made as manager of the boutique." She threw up a hand, stopping Mary Claire before she could even offer. "And, no, I won't accept a loan from you."

Mary Claire pressed her lips together and went back to her shelling. "I still don't understand why you got stuck with all of Roger's debt."

Leighanna heaved a sigh. "Because we were married. Because the debts were in both our names. Because Texas is a community property state. And because Roger is a jerk and refuses to pay them."

"Couldn't you just declare bankruptcy?"

"I could...but I won't. It's bad enough that I have to suffer because of Roger's shortcomings. I won't allow anyone else to suffer, too."

"So, you're just going to work your fingers to the bone until they're all paid off?"

"If it takes that. But the bonus at the end is that my name will be clear and my credit standing will be good again. That makes all the hard work worthwhile."

Not wanting to think about her debts anymore, it was much too pretty a day for such morbid thoughts, Leighanna closed her eyes and lifted her face to the sun. "I see why you love it here so much. The air is clean, the sky is clear—"

"And there's not a traffic jam in sight," Mary Claire finished for her. "Heaven, isn't it?"

"What's heaven?"

Mary Claire and Leighanna both looked up to see Harley, Mary Claire's fiancé, strolling down the brick walk toward them. Leighanna could see the love in the man's eyes as he looked at Mary Claire and felt just the tiniest stab of envy. She'd met Harley on her first visit to Temptation and had immediately liked the man. Beyond the fact that he was drop-dead handsome, he seemed to adore Mary Claire and her children, and that alone was enough to win Leighanna's approval of him.

Smiling, Mary Claire lifted her face for Harley's kiss. "Temptation." She patted the spot next to her on the step. "Join us. Leighanna was just singing the praises of her new home."

Harley chuckled as he dropped down beside Mary Claire. "Tough night at work?" he asked, gesturing to the pan of water where Leighanna soaked.

Leighanna frowned. "In more ways than one."

Mary Claire bit back a smile. "I think your friend Hank made a bad impression with Leighanna."

Harley reared back, looking at Leighanna in surprise. "Hank?"

"Yes, Hank," Leighanna said sourly. "Do you know that he had the audacity to ask me to kiss him?"

"Did you?" Harley and Mary Claire asked at the same time.

Leighanna reared back, looking at them in surprise. "Well, of course I didn't! The man's a lecher!"

Mary Claire bit back a smile and Harley nearly choked on a laugh, but both remained silent.

"Well, he is!" Leighanna cried indignantly. "Every time I turned around, he was there, touching me or brushing up against me." She shuddered, remembering.

"Most women would kill to have Hank pay 'em that much attention," Harley offered quietly.

Leighanna rolled her eyes. "Well, as far as I'm concerned, they can have him. The man has a one-track mind. Sex!''

Leighanna tried the door and found it unlocked. ''Hank?'' she called hesitantly as she pushed open the door. ''Are you here?'' When he didn't answer, she hesitated a moment, then with a shrug, stepped inside and closed the door behind her.

Heading straight for the bar, she tossed her purse behind it and grabbed a clean towel to tuck into her jeans. If she'd learned anything from her first night at work, it was the proper apparel for a waitress in a place like The End of the Road. Today she'd worn jeans and a *washable* cotton shirt. She'd already ruined one silk blouse at The End of the Road and wasn't anxious to sacrifice another.

She caught a glimpse of herself in the mirror behind the bar and fought back a shudder. Always a woman who took pride in her appearance, her current state of dress was somewhat depressing. As the manager of the clothing boutique in Houston, the image she had projected had been important. Since the owners of the boutique had included a generous discount on all the clothes she purchased there, doing so had been easy.

Glancing down at her feet, she frowned. The running shoes were certainly not a fashion statement, that was for sure, but hopefully, with their help, she wouldn't need to soak her feet again.

With a sigh, she glanced at the clock behind the bar...and smiled. Four-thirty. She'd purposefully arrived early, just to spite Hank. Too bad he wasn't around so that she could gloat.

Humming softly, she dragged the chairs from the tables, then refilled the salt and pepper shakers, just as she'd done the night before. When Hank still hadn't appeared by the time she'd finished, she glanced around, trying to decide what she should do next. One look at the filthy front windows gave her the answer she needed. Taking the bucket, she filled it with water and a heavy dose of vinegar, grabbed a couple of clean rags and headed for the front door.

Once outside, she parked the bucket beneath a window and stepped back, folding her arms beneath her breasts as she studied the building. The structure itself was old, probably built more than fifty years before, and was constructed of native limestone. Only two windows faced the front of the narrow structure, but the double doors situated between them each sported a glass. A faded sign stretched above the door. The End of the Road, she silently read.

It was certainly that, she admitted, glancing around at its remote location. Situated at the edge of town, the building stood over two hundred feet from the main road. Fronted by a gravel parking lot, and protected on three sides by thick stands of cedar, the bar seemed to have sprouted from the rocky ground itself. Thick clumps of cactus cropped up here and there along the fence line bordering the parking lot, and a tangle of weeds and vines grew in the narrow strip of ground between the gravel lot and the building itself.

The place could use a face-lift in the worst sort of way, she thought, frowning. The eaves needed painting, the front doors could definitely use a new coat of varnish, and those weeds should be replaced with a strip of hedge. A spot or two of color wouldn't hurt, either, she mused, thinking a pot of geraniums at either side of the entrance would certainly add charm. And charm would bring in more customers, increasing the bar's business, and hopefully her tips.

Sighing, Leighanna stooped and picked up a rag. She knew without asking that even if she found the courage to suggest the improvements to Hank, he'd never implement them. The man obviously had a problem accepting change. His comments to her about all the strangers who'd flocked to Temptation proved that.

Sighing again, Leighanna dipped the rag into the bucket. Washing the windows wouldn't help the bar's appearance much, but at least it was a start. Besides, she told herself, it would pass the time while she waited for Hank to show up, and maybe even impress him with her resourcefulness.

Enjoying the feel of the sun on her back, she put her hand in motion on the door's window and her elbow behind her work. When she'd cleaned them both, she went back inside and dragged out a bar stool to stand on in order to reach the high windows that flanked the doors.

Leighanna finished the first and stepped down to admire her work. The transformation was staggering. The window gleamed like new glass, catching the sun's rays and reflecting it back. Motivated by her accomplishment, she dragged the bucket and stool beneath the second window.

Just as she made the last satisfying swipe, she heard tires spitting gravel behind her and glanced over her shoulder to see a truck speeding across the lot straight for her. Her movement made the tall stool rock beneath her, and she slapped a hand against the window to brace herself.

The truck slid to a stop, shooting up a cloud of white dust, and Leighanna frowned, thinking of the windows she'd just cleaned. Hank swung down from the truck and charged for her, his face twisted in a scowl.

"What in the hell do you think you're doing?" he asked, grinding to a stop at the side of her stool.

"I'm cleaning the windows," she said, surprised by his anger.

He grabbed her by the waist and hauled her down. Caught off guard, Leighanna planted her hands against his chest to keep from crumpling when her feet slammed against solid ground.

"I didn't ask you to clean the damn windows," he snarled.

His mouth was set in a thin tight line, his eyes dark and threatening. For the life of her, Leighanna couldn't imagine what she'd done to anger him so.

"No, you didn't," she said nervously. "But you weren't here and I'd already done everything else and the windows needed cleaning, so I cleaned them."

His jaw tightened and a muscle twitched beneath his eye. When his fingers continued to cut into her waist, she decided she'd had enough of his rotten attitude. "If you don't mind," she said, and gave his chest a shove. "I'd appreciate it if you'd let me go."

His fingers cut a little deeper and his eyes narrowed to dangerous slits. "And what if I do mind?" he asked.

Leighanna's eyes flipped wide. Hank saw the fear in them, and it shamed him to think he had put it there. He'd never frightened a woman before, had never used force on one, either, for that matter, had never needed to. But there was something about this woman that seemed to bring out the worst in him.

"It doesn't matter if *you* mind or not," she cried indignantly, "because *I* do!" She pushed a little more insistently. "Now let me go, I've got work to do before customers start arriving."

But Hank wasn't ready to let her go just yet. He hadn't

expected her to show up for work again, not after what he'd put her through the night before. Then to find her there, swaying like a suction cup, dashboard ornament on that damn rickety stool, washing windows...well, it had just about given him a heart attack. All he could think about was that fragile body of hers lying in a crumpled heap on the ground, those delicate bones shattered beyond repair, and not a soul within a three-mile radius of the bar to hear her calls for help.

Knowing that she was safe didn't loosen his hold on her, though, for now with her close like this, with her womanly scent teasing his senses and the feel of her soft flesh curving beneath his palms, the fear slowly subsided, leaving in its place nothing but a keen awareness.

"There's time, yet," he murmured, and enjoyed watching the indignant thrust of her chin. He forced himself to soften his hold on her until his hands merely rested in the curve of her waist. He dipped his face a hair lower, just close enough to warm her lips with his breath. "You've got dirt on your cheek," he said, his voice husky.

Leighanna immediately lifted a fist to her cheek and scrubbed. "Where?"

He caught her hand and forced it back to his chest. "Right here." He lifted a finger to her cheek and whisked softly, his face drifting closer, then closer still, until it was his lips that brushed her cheek instead of his fingers. His mouth opened and his tongue arced out, sweeping like wet velvet across her cheek.

Leighanna sucked in a sharp breath, fisting her hands in the fabric of his shirt as her knees turned the consistency of wet noodles. Now she understood why Harley had said most women would kill to have Hank pay attention to them. The man was a master at seduction.

She could feel herself weakening, falling deeper and deeper under his spell as his tongue and lips teased. "Please," she begged, her voice little more than a whimper.

"Please, what?" he murmured huskily.

But before she could ask him to stop, his mouth slipped to cover hers. Leighanna almost wept at the feel of those lips on hers. Strong and commanding, they moved against hers in a most satisfying way, while his thumbs stroked persuasively at her lower ribs.

She knew she was weak, spineless, susceptible when confronted with a man's seductive charm. Her years with Roger had certainly proven that.

How many times had Roger come to her, whispering sweet nothings in her ear and cuddling up to her while he tried to wheedle money out of her? She'd always been a sucker for affection. Raised by a father who didn't have a clue about the needs of a young girl, she'd never received any. Roger had known her weakness, knew just the right buttons to push to get what he wanted from her.

The thought of Roger's manipulations dragged her from beneath Hank's spell. She set her jaw and firmed her lips beneath his. He might not want money from her as Roger had, but he wanted something. That was obvious in the seductive prodding of his tongue against her lips...and she wouldn't, no matter how strong the temptation to remain in his arms, allow herself to fall prey to a man's charm again.

Lifting her foot, she brought it down hard across his instep. He released her with a yelp of pain and hopped around on one foot while he cradled in his hands the one she'd stomped.

"Why in the hell'd you do that for?" he asked incredulously. "You could've broken my damn foot!"

Leighanna folded her arms beneath her breasts. "You're lucky I didn't aim a little higher."

Hank's eyes widened in surprise while his grip on his foot loosened. "Why, you little hellcat," he murmured.

He couldn't have called her anything that would have pleased her more. Leighanna Farrow would never again be any man's doormat! She snatched up the bucket. "If you're smart, you'll remember that before you try to make another pass at me." She jerked open the door. "Get the stool," she ordered firmly, pointing a stiff finger at the stool beneath the window. "We've got work to do."

Hank's chest swelled in anger. "I think you're forgetting who's the boss around here."

Leighanna refused to bend under his threatening look. She'd done enough bending in her life. "No, I haven't forgotten, but it appears one of us needs to keep an eye on the business. You obviously don't care." With that she stepped through the door with a deliberate toss of her blond hair and let the door slam closed behind her.

Didn't care about his business! Hank snatched up the stool and jerked open the door, following her into the bar. "And just exactly what is that supposed to mean?" he asked, slamming the stool down on four legs as he stomped after her toward the kitchen.

Leighanna calmly tipped over the bucket and emptied its contents down the drain. "Exactly what I said. You don't care about your business."

"That's a damn lie!"

She set the bucket on the floor by the sink and brushed past him on her way to the bar. "It isn't. If you did, you'd take better care of the place."

Hank followed her. "I take care of my business!"

She wheeled, and he fell back a step to keep from

slamming into her. "Do you?" she asked, arching a neatly shaped brow.

"Well, hell, yes!"

"Then why are you letting this place fall down around you?"

Hank looked at her in dismay. "It's not falling down!"

"Sure it is." She stepped to the wall and tapped a manicured nail at a spot of chipped plaster. "This for instance. How long has this been this way?"

Hank frowned. "The walls look the same as when I bought the place."

"And how long has that been?"

"Six years."

She dipped her chin and looked at him from beneath her eyebrows, the smirk on her mouth telling him that his answer only proved her point.

"Well, I sure as hell don't hear my customers complaining," he said defensively.

"That's because they don't have a choice. Yours is the only bar in town. But if another opened," she quickly added, before he could interrupt, "which is a strong possibility with all the people who keep swarming through Temptation, then you might very well lose your customers."

Her statement momentarily stripped Hank's tongue of the scathing remark he'd been about to make. He'd never thought about the possibility of competition. The End of the Road had been the only bar in Temptation for as long as he could remember.

Before he could gather his wits enough to respond, the door opened and Cody Fipes, Temptation's sheriff, strolled in.

"Hey!" Cody called, hooking a thumb over his shoulder. "Who cleaned the windows? Had to put on my sunglasses to kill the glare."

Leighanna turned to Hank, folding her arms beneath her breasts. "See?" she said, smiling sweetly. "Someone did notice."

It rankled more than Hank wanted to admit, but Cody wasn't the only one who commented on the clean windows that night at the bar. Even old Will Miller, Temptation's one-and-only barber and the crankiest SOB in town, noticed the change and even found a smile for Leighanna when he'd learned she was responsible for the work.

Hank bit back an oath. Wasn't nothin' wrong with the looks of The End of the Road, he told himself as he scooped coins from the cash register drawer onto his open palm. Hell, business was good, always had been, and nobody'd ever complained about the appearance of the place before...at least not before Leighanna had taken it upon herself to clean those damned windows.

It was all her fault, he told himself as he started sorting the coins into piles by denomination. He'd never thought twice about what his bar looked like. He'd been too damn busy serving drinks and slapping hamburgers on a grill to pay it any mind...at least not until Leighanna had shot off her sassy mouth.

But as a result of her comments, earlier, when the sunshine had been gleaming through those windows she'd cleaned, the plaster on the old interior walls had appeared to him a little more crusty and duller than they had before. Even the mirror behind the bar seemed intent on rubbing Hank's nose in his neglect by reflecting the chipped plaster back at him when his back was turned to the open room.

Angrily, he scraped a handful of quarters into his hand to count. "What else do you think is wrong with the place?" he muttered disagreeably.

Startled by the unexpected question, Leighanna straightened from her mopping and used her wrist to push her hair from her face as she turned to look at him. His head was bent over the coins, but she could tell by the way one side of his mouth curled down that he was still irritated by all the attention the clean windows had drawn.

And that is just too bad, she thought peevishly. Because she was right. He *had* neglected the building.

"The eaves need painting, the doors need revarnishing and it wouldn't hurt to freshen up the sign." She started to mention the pots of geraniums, but decided she'd better not push her luck. "And that's just on the outside," she said before going back to her mopping.

His head snapped up. "And what's wrong with the inside? Other than the plaster," he quickly added before she could rub his nose in that again.

Leighanna sighed and drew the mop up, folding her hands over the top of its handle. "Well, for starters, the tabletops are a disgrace. They've been scrubbed so much there is nothing left of their finish but raw wood. It's all but impossible to get the stains off them."

He hunched his shoulders defensively. "I can't afford to replace every damn table in the place."

"You wouldn't have to. You could either refinish them, or maybe even use tablecloths to cover them. A bit of color certainly wouldn't hurt."

"Tablecloths!" He snorted and slapped a ten dollar stack of quarters onto the bar. "If you had your way, you'd turn this place into a damn tearoom."

"Tables in a tearoom are covered with linen and lace. I was thinking more in the line of checkered oilcloths."

Hank cocked his head to look at her in disgust. "Checkered?"

"Yes," she said, hoping she could hold his interest long enough to convince him. "Preferably red and white. It would carry out your country motif."

"What the hell's a motif?"

"You know," she said, fluttering her hand at him. "Theme."

It was all Hank could do to keep from rolling his eyes. A country motif, for God's sake! As if he'd actually had a theme in mind when he'd opened The End of the Road for business.

But then he remembered the compliments the clean windows had drawn and Leighanna's warning that somebody might move into Temptation and open a new bar to compete against him. He'd already heard the rumors about a couple who were moving to town to open a clothing store. For all he knew, someone could very well be planning to open a bar. Hank knew he was stubborn, but he certainly wasn't a fool.

He levered a pile of dimes into a stack. "I suppose if a person were of a mind," he muttered, "they could pick up something like that over at Carter's Mercantile."

Surprised that he'd even consider her suggestion, Leighanna took a hesitant step toward him. "I could do it for you. In fact, I could measure the tables and cut the cloth myself."

He hesitated only a second. "All right, do it then. But I don't want anything checkered. Stick with a solid color, something that won't show dirt. You can tell Mrs. Martin over at the Mercantile to charge it to my account."

The man was so bullheaded, Leighanna thought in

frustration. Checkered cloth would look a hundred times better than any solid. But at least he was willing to make a change. "I'll go first thing in the morning and have the cloths on the table by tomorrow night."

He waved a negligent hand, then went back to his counting. "Whatever."

Bracing herself for an explosion, she squared her shoulders. "I will expect to be paid for my time."

He didn't look up, but kept sifting through the coins on the bar. "Fine. Keep up with the time you spend and turn it in Saturday with your regular hours."

Since he didn't balk at the idea of paying her for extra work, Leighanna decided to go for broke. "I can paint, too."

His head jerked up, his brown eyes slamming into hers. "Paint?"

Leighanna swallowed hard. "Yes. I could revarnish the front doors and paint the building's eaves for you, if you like."

Hank dropped his gaze to the delicate manicured hands that still clutched the mop handle, then back to her face. "You're kidding, right?"

Leighanna stiffened her spine. "I assure you I can handle the job. My father was a paint contractor. I know what work is required."

He just shook his head, chuckling. "And when would you find the time? You're already putting in a forty-hour week here as a waitress."

"We're closed on Sundays. I could do the work then."

Hank sobered, slowly becoming aware of the earnestness in her expression...and remembered the desperation in her voice when she'd first asked for the waitressing job. At the time she'd told him she needed the money. Since she was willing to work seven days a week, and at a job most men avoided, he figured she must need it pretty damn bad.

Frowning, he gave his head a brisk nod, telling himself that he wasn't doing her any favors. She'd more than earn the hourly wage he would pay her. "All right. The job's yours. I've got an account at the hardware store. Charge whatever supplies you need and tell 'em to send me a bill." He shifted to lift up the tray in the cash drawer and scooped out a key. He tossed it to her and she caught it between her palms. "You'll need a key. And don't lose it," he warned. "There are a couple of ladders in the shed out back. The key opens that door, as well. Use whatever you need. And for God's sake, brace the ladder so you don't fall and break your neck."

"Can I help you?"

Leighanna glanced up to find a gray-haired bear of a woman, chugging down the cluttered aisle toward her and knew she had to be the owner of the Mercantile, Mrs. Martin. She offered the woman a tentative smile. "Well, yes, as a matter of fact you can. I was looking for oil-cloth."

Mrs. Martin tilted her head back, peering at Leighanna through smudged reading glasses perched on the end of her nose. "You're Leighanna, aren't you? Mary Claire's friend?"

"Yes. I am."

"Thought so." She gestured for Leighanna to follow her as she shuffled down the aisle toward the back of the store. "Did you find yourself a job?"

Leighanna bit back a smile. It seemed Mary Claire was right about Mrs. Martin. She kept track of all of Temptation's goings on. "Yes, ma'am, I did. I'm working as a waitress at The End of the Road."

The woman stopped and whirled, her walruslike brows arching high on her wrinkled forehead while her glasses slipped even further down her nose. "You?" she asked in amazement. "Waitressing at The End of the Road?"

Leighanna firmed her lips in irritation. She was a little tired of everyone thinking she was incapable of handling the job at The End of the Road. "Yes, me."

"Well, I'll be..." The woman let the words drift off before she started shaking her head and wagging a finger beneath Leighanna's nose. "You be careful around that old Hank Braden. He's a rounder, that one, and wouldn't know how to treat a well-bred lady like yourself."

Leighanna had to catch herself before she laughed. Not that she doubted Hank was a womanizer. She'd seen enough proof of that for herself. But as to her being well-bred? Now that was worth a laugh. Her father was nothing but a mean-spirited paint contractor from the wrong side of Houston, with a heart as cold as a block of ice. And her mother had been such a mouse she had died in order to escape a marriage she didn't have the courage to end.

Leighanna liked to believe she'd inherited nothing from her father. Her heart, she thought, if anything, was too warm and full of feeling. But from her mother? Well, maybe she'd inherited one or two of the mouse genes. But that certainly didn't mean she was as weak as her mother! She'd proved that when she'd found the courage to divorce Roger, thus removing herself from a disastrous marriage, and had proved it even more so when she'd left Houston for Temptation.

But Mrs. Martin didn't have to know any of that. Leighanna was determined to put her past behind her.

"Thank you for the warning," she said instead. "But I can handle Hank Braden. Now about that oilcloth," she said, hoping to refocus Mrs. Martin's attention on the task at hand. "I'm making tablecloths for the bar, and I'll need about forty-two yards."

"Tablecloths for The End of the Road?" Mrs. Martin parroted.

"Yes, tablecloths," Leighanna replied firmly.

Mrs. Martin eyed her for a moment, then surprised Leighanna by tossing back her head and cackling like a chicken that had just laid a prize egg. "Well, I'll be hog-tied!" she said, her breath wheezing out of her. "Table-cloths at The End of the Road. Who'd have ever thought?" She slapped Leighanna on the back, nearly sending her to her knees. "I believe you might just be able to handle old Hank, after all." Still chortling, she gave Leighanna a push toward the back of the store.

"That Hank's a wild one," she said, wagging her head. "Always was. Had to be, I guess, in order to survive, what with him not having a daddy to keep him in line."

"His father is deceased?" Leighanna asked, unable to suppress her curiosity.

"Wouldn't know whether he's deceased or not. Hank's mother never knew who fathered the boy. She was too busy slipping out of one bed and into another to notice, I guess. After Hank was born, half the time she'd even forget to take him with her when she made the shift." She made a clucking sound with her tongue. "Poor little fellow. Fended for himself for the most part. Amazing, really, that he turned out as well as he did."

Leighanna felt a pang of sympathy for the little boy Hank had once been...then just as quickly, pushed it back. She wouldn't feel sorry for a man like Hank Braden. He was a womanizer, stubborn as a mule and a little too good-looking for his own good. He didn't deserve her pity.

Mrs. Martin stopped before a rack of shelves that climbed all the way to the ceiling. She waved a hand at the bolts of fabric neatly stacked on one of the upper shelves, sending the loose skin on her under arm flapping. Solids in white, black and a dull navy sat propped against each other. "Keep all my bolts of fabrics and notions and such back here in the corner out of the way of grimy fingers. What color will you be needin'?"

Leighanna eyed them a moment, remembering Hank's instructions to select something dark that wouldn't show stains. That certainly ruled out the white. But she knew that the black and navy would do nothing but add more gloom to the already dreary bar.

Impulsively, she swung her finger to point at a bolt of red-and-white-checkered cloth tucked almost out of sight. She drew in a deep, fortifying breath. "That one."

Three

Leighanna knelt in the shade of the old live oak in Mary Claire's backyard with her knees buried in cool grass, her head bent over the bolt of red-and-white checkered cloth spread out in front of her, while she painstakingly cut another square. A neat stack of folded squares, already cut from the bolt, lay on the grass at her side. Behind her, propped on an old board balanced between two sawhorses, a line of red, spray-painted tuna cans dried in the sun. In a box beneath the sawhorses, fifteen lantern globes nested in shredded newspaper, sharing the space with fifteen long, tapered white candles. A five-pound bag of sand rested against the side of the box.

Leighanna made the last snip in the oilcloth and sank back on her heels, pressing a hand at the ache in her lower back. Cutting the cloth on Mary Claire's kitchen table would have been easier, she knew, but being outdoors certainly outweighed whatever inconveniences she'd endured. While living in Houston, the closest she had come to enjoying the outdoors had been in lying by the pool at the apartment complex where she'd lived.

She tipped back her head, letting the sunshine—dappled by the lacework of leaves overhead—warm her skin. God, how she loved it here! She'd never lived in a real house, not even as a child. She'd always lived in apartment buildings or duplexes, where trees were simply ornaments and the only flowers in sight swung from baskets suspended from high balconies or eaves.

She let her chin drop slowly until her gaze rested on the picket fence surrounding Mary Claire's house...and her heart squeezed in her chest. She'd always dreamed of living in a house, a real house, with trees in the yard big enough to offer shade on a sunny afternoon, where a profusion of flowers that changed with the seasons filled the beds...and all of it framed by a white picket fence.

With a sigh, she pushed to her feet. Someday, she promised herself, she'd live that dream, but for now she had work to do and debts to pay off. She crossed to the sawhorses and placed a tentative finger to one of the cans and found the paint dry. All that was left for her to do now was to cart her supplies to the bar and set it all up.

At the thought, she caught her lower lip between her teeth. What would Hank do when he discovered what she had done? she wondered. Would he be angry enough to fire her?

She gave herself a firm shake. He wouldn't fire her, she told herself. It wasn't as if she'd bought all these things just to spite him. The idea to make the centerpieces had been an inspiration, coming to her when she'd found the lantern globes on a discount table at Mrs. Martin's store. She knew that she had overstepped her bounds in purchasing the globes. After all, Hank had only given her

permission to buy the oilcloth. But she also knew the
centerpieces would look fantastic sitting in the center of
each of the red-and-white-checkered cloths. She banked
on Hank realizing that, too, once he saw them in place.

Besides, she told herself, the cost in making them was
hardly anything the man could quibble about. The empty
tuna cans had been donated by Mary Claire. God love
her, Leighanna thought with a soft laugh. Mary Claire,
once a die-hard city girl, had turned into a frugal country
woman after her move to Temptation, saving everything
for which she thought she might one day have a use. It
had taken some talking, but Leighanna had finally convinced Mary Claire that The End of the Road needed the
cans more than she did.

The candles were the only costly item. And if Hank
threw a fit when he received the bill for them from Mrs.
Martin—well, he wouldn't, she told herself. Once he saw
the tables covered with the red-and-white-checkered
cloths and the candles glowing inside the lantern globes,
he'd see for himself what a difference the centerpieces
made.

The sound of an engine's roar interrupted her thoughts.
Shielding her eyes against the sun, she turned toward the
sound and saw a tractor bumping across the pasture toward the fence. Smiling, she lifted a hand in a wave,
knowing that it was Harley coming to Mary Claire's for
lunch.

Anxious to get to the bar and get everything set up,
she quickly tossed the scissors into the box, then stooped
and gathered the cut cloths into her arms.

"Hey, Leighanna!" Harley called as he swung down
from his tractor. "What're you doing, getting ready for
some target practice?"

Leighanna glanced at Harley over her shoulder then

followed his gaze to the line of cans perched on the board. She laughed. "No, but I might need some if—" She was about to say she might need a little target practice if Hank came gunning for her when he found out what she'd done, but her explanation died on her lips when she saw a second man climb down from the tractor's cab.

Hank! All her self-assurances that he would approve of what she'd done suddenly vanished when confronted with the hard, disapproving lines of his face. Dressed in worn jeans and a cotton T-shirt that hugged his muscled chest and arms, he cut an imposing, if breathtaking figure as he strode toward her.

Harley didn't seem to notice her sudden uneasiness. "Mary Claire in the kitchen?" he asked as he paused at the makeshift table.

Leighanna tightened her arms around the tablecloths, hoping to disguise their color from Hank as he came to a stop alongside Harley. "Y-yes," she stammered. "Lunch should be just about ready."

"Good. I'm starving." Harley swung around and headed for the house, leaving Hank and Leighanna to follow.

Hank hitched his hands at his hips and frowned at Leighanna. "What are you doing here?"

Leighanna nervously wet her lips. "I live here. Mary Claire is a friend of mine." Disgusted at her nervousness and a little irritated that he would question her presence there, she tossed his question back at him. "What are *you* doing here?"

He lifted a shoulder in a shrug. "Harley needed help with his hay. I've been raking while he baled." Still wearing the frown, he nodded toward the cloths she held. "Are those the tablecloths for the bar?"

"Yes," she replied, and hugged them protectively against her breasts.

His frown deepened. "Thought I told you to buy a solid color?"

"You did, but the selection at the Mercantile was limited. Mrs. Martin only had white, black and a dull navy. I thought the checkered fabric the best choice."

He merely grunted, then gestured toward the cans. "What's all this?"

Here it comes, Leighanna thought. The moment of reckoning. She took a deep breath, her nerves beginning to dance again beneath her skin. "Bases for centerpieces. I found these lantern globes on the discount table at the Mercantile and thought how wonderful they'd look on the tables with a candle lit inside. They cost almost nothing to make," she hurried to explain as Hank hunkered down to examine the contents of the box at her feet. "Mary Claire donated the cans and the paint, and the cost of the sand was minimal. The candles were the only true expense. I'm sorry I didn't ask you first, and if you want to dock my pay for the expense—"

Hank glanced up at her, his eyes narrowed against the sun at her back. Dust powdered his face and darkened the grooves at the corners of his eyes. He stood, his gaze still on hers, aligning his body almost flush with hers. He brought with him the mingling scents of sweat and sunshine and the sweet scent of freshly mown hay. Bits of it still clung to his hair and his T-shirt.

Cleaned up, he was mouthwateringly handsome. Drenched in sweat, and with dirt streaking those perfect features, he was even more ruggedly so. The sight of him, the very smell of him, robbed Leighanna of her guilt over the purchases she'd made and left her with only the memory of those muscled arms wrapped around her, the devastating power of that frowning mouth pressed over hers.

It was crazy. She knew it was. Especially since she was the one who had ended that last kiss. But she had the most insane urge to close the distance between them, to offer herself to him, to feel again that muscled wall of chest pressed seductively against her breasts. To feel those work-roughened hands of his moving against her skin. To taste the sweat that beaded his upper lip and to savor the salt from it on her tongue.

Horrified by her own thoughts, she fell back a step before she could give in to the urge.

Hank brought his hands to his hips as she moved away, his lips twisting into a scowl. "What is it with you?" he asked in frustration. "Every time I get near you, you start doing this little nervous two-step. Are you afraid of me or something?"

"N-no," she said, and stopped herself before she could take another step in retreat.

"Well, what is it then?"

Leighanna struggled to think of an excuse for her actions. "I...I just don't want to give you the wrong impression," she finally said.

His forehead furrowed. "What wrong impression?"

"That I'm...w-well, that I'm leading you on, or something."

"Leading me on!" he echoed, choking back a laugh. "And how, in the name of God, would I get an idea like that with you dancing away from me every time I get within ten feet of you?" When she didn't say anything, his eyes narrowed in suspicion. "You are afraid of me, aren't you?"

"No!" She immediately regretted the speed and force of her response, knowing by the satisfied purse of his lips that he knew she lied. "Well, maybe a little," she amended reluctantly.

He took a step toward her, robbing her of the space she'd managed to place between them. "I don't usually frighten women."

Leighanna stiffened, refusing to let him see her fear. "Perhaps that's because you treat them differently than you do me."

"And how do I treat you?"

"You frown at me all the time, and nothing I do ever seems to please you."

His left eyebrow arched appraisingly as he took his gaze on a slow journey down her front. He returned his gaze to hers. "Oh, you please me all right," he replied, a teasing grin chipping at the corner of his mouth.

"That's exactly what I'm talking about," she said, her chin coming up in that regal lift that tended to drive Hank a little crazy. "You take unfair advantage of your role as my employer."

"Unfair advantage?" he repeated, trying not to laugh at her prim tone.

That he would find this discussion amusing made Leighanna's chest swell in indignation. "Yes, unfair advantage," she repeated firmly.

He studied her a moment, then lifted a hand to her cheek and caught a stray tendril of hair. Lazily he tucked it behind her ear, leaving his fingers to curl at her ear's delicate shell.

"And how do I do that?" he asked, his voice taking on a low, seductive drawl.

His touch was gentle, almost tender, but burned like fire against Leighanna's skin, weakening her ability to keep her mind on the point she was trying to make. "You...you...you kissed me," she finally managed to say, and felt her cheeks burn in humiliation when his lips curved into a full-blown smile.

"A kiss isn't supposed to frighten. It's supposed to please." He took a step closer, slipping his hand from her ear to cup the back of her neck, and sent shivers chasing down her spine. "Here, let me show you."

Her eyes widened in alarm as his face lowered to hers. She would have stopped him, she knew she would, but just before his lips reached hers, he veered, catching her totally off guard as he captured instead the tender lobe of her ear. His teeth nipped, his lips soothed, and she felt her knees weakening, her breath growing shorter by the second.

"See?" he murmured, his breath blowing warm against her neck where he nuzzled. "That isn't anything to be afraid of, now is it?"

"No, but—"

Before she could finish that *but,* Hank shifted again, bringing his lips to hers. At the first contact, Leighanna tensed and willed herself to remain unmoved, remembering the devastation and the seductive power of his last kiss. But though her resolve remained steadfast, it seemed her body had a mind of its own. Slowly, muscle by muscle, she melted against him as his lips moved like magic across hers. The tablecloths she held pressed against her breasts slipped from her grasp, and her arms dropped bonelessly to hang slack at her sides.

Quickly closing the space the tablecloths had once filled, Hank gathered her waist in the curve of his arm and pulled her hard against him. He knew that she was right, that he didn't treat her like he did other women. But she wasn't like any other woman he'd ever known. She was a paradox: classy as a New York model with her slender figure and delicate features, yet she worked like a mule at whatever menial tasks he tossed her way. Half the time she looked as if she'd jump out of her skin if he so much as said "boo" to her, while the other half she was all temper and sass.

So maybe he did treat her differently. But damned if he took unfair advantage of her. She'd wanted that first kiss as badly as he.... She just didn't want to admit it. And that was what he wanted to prove.

But something happened when her body met his, when the nipples of her small breasts stabbed against his sweat-dampened chest, when that soft whimper escaped her lips as he'd thrust his tongue into the sweetness of her mouth. A knot had formed in his stomach and an ache had grown in his groin...and his heart had done a slow three-sixty-degree turn. Even as he drew the kiss out, deepening it, he felt his heart right itself and slam against his chest into a pounding beat.

He wanted her. And for more than just a kiss. He wanted her naked on the ground beneath him, right here, right now, writhing, her legs wrapped around his waist, his manhood buried so deep inside her that it would take hours for them to separate. He wanted to hear her cries as he drove her over the edge. He wanted to feel the pulsations of her body around him as she lost control.

He wanted to hold her and never let her go.

And that's what scared him.

Oh, not that he wanted her. He'd wanted women before. Had never had a problem finding a willing one to bed. But none of those women had ever aroused him the way this one did. He'd never been tempted to hold on to one too long, not like he wanted to do with Leighanna. In the past, he'd always been more likely to just give and take a little pleasure with a woman then give her an affectionate pat on the butt when they went their separate ways.

And that's what scared him more than anything else. He didn't think that one night of sex was going to be enough. Not with Leighanna.

Knowing this and not liking it one damn bit, he purposefully softened the kiss, then slowly withdrew, careful to keep his expression blank as he let his gaze meet hers. The blue eyes that met his were glazed with passion, the cheeks flushed, the lips swollen...and he was tempted to drag her into his arms again.

Fighting the desire to do something he'd more than likely regret, he took a step back and forced a teasing grin to his mouth. "See?" he said, lifting his hands palms up. "That wasn't so bad, was it?"

Bad? It was anything but bad, Leighanna thought numbly, her blood still racing like fire through her veins. *Tempting, seductive, world shattering* all seemed much more appropriate terms for what she had just experienced. But Hank's casual, almost offhand remark about something that left her wanting nothing but more of the same infuriated Leighanna. She sucked in a raw breath and opened her hand at her side.

His indifferent stance made Hank vulnerable to the force of the hand that suddenly streaked out and slapped the side of his face. Reeling, he staggered back a step, covering the already reddening cheek with his palm as he stared at Leighanna in openmouthed surprise. Her lips were still swollen from his bruising kiss, her cheeks still flushed, but the passion that had glazed her eyes before had disappeared, leaving those blue depths the color of fired steel.

"What was that for?" he asked incredulously.

Her hand still stinging from the force of the slap,

Leighanna glared at him. "I warned you once," she said, fighting to keep the tremble from her voice as she stooped and scraped the dropped cloths back into her arms. "Next time you better think twice before kissing me." Straightening, she glanced up and the anger drained out of her at the sight of the angry red handprint she'd left on his face.

She'd never struck anyone before. The thought that she had done so now, and to her boss no less, set her insides quivering. She swallowed hard and raised her gaze higher until her eyes met his. Fear stabbed through at her at the lethal look she found in those brown depths. "I suppose you're going to fire me now," she said, trying to keep the tears that threatened at bay.

His gaze continued to bore through her. "I could," he agreed slowly. "You've certainly given me cause. But I'm not," he added, surprising her. "Like I told you before, us kissing has nothing to do with you working for me." He continued to stare at her, his expression turning thoughtful. "You know what?" he said slowly. "I don't think it's me you're afraid of at all. I think it's what my kiss does to you that scares you." He lifted a hand to run a thumb along her bottom lip. "But don't worry," he promised softly. "I'll take heed of your warning. Next time it'll be *you* kissing me."

With that, he turned on his heel and strode for the house, whistling merrily under his breath.

"Sure smells good," Hank said as he stepped into Mary Claire's kitchen. "Did y'all leave anything for the hired help?"

Sitting across from the door, Mary Claire waved a hand toward the opposite side of the table. "There's plenty." She pushed from her chair to greet him. "You must be—"

"Hank," he said, grinning. "And you must be Mary Claire."

"Yes," she murmured, unable to keep from staring at the red mark on his face. "What happened to you?"

Hank chuckled ruefully as he touched three fingers to his still-smarting cheek. "I ran into Leighanna's hand."

Mary Claire's mouth dropped open. "She slapped you?"

Hank shrugged. "I guess you could call it that."

Mary Claire wagged her head, unable to believe her friend capable of such a violent act. "You're teasing me, aren't you? Leighanna would never lift a hand against anyone. She's much too gentle a person for that."

Hank snorted as he dropped down in a chair opposite Harley and pulled a napkin across his lap. "Are we talking about the same person, here? The Leighanna I know is a little hellcat. The last time I crossed her she nearly broke my damn foot."

"Leighanna?" Mary Claire cried in dismay.

"Yes, Leighanna."

Unable to think of anything that would push Leighanna to such lengths, Mary Claire trailed him to the table. "What did you do to cross her?"

Hank shrugged as he reached for a bowl of mashed potatoes. "Just gave her a little kiss, that's all."

"A little kiss," Mary Claire repeated, casting a furtive glance Harley's way. Harley just shrugged a shoulder and dipped his head over his plate and shoveled another forkful of chicken-fried steak into his mouth, obviously not wanting to get involved in this discussion. Knowing she was on her own on this one, Mary Claire turned her gaze back on Hank. Fully aware of his reputation around town, she narrowed an eye at him. "And did Leighanna *want* you to kiss her?"

"Sure she did," Hank replied, defensively. "Though I'm sure she'd never admit it."

"Then what makes you think she wanted you to kiss her?" Mary Claire asked pointedly.

Hank paused a minute, a heaping spoonful of potatoes suspended halfway between the bowl and his plate. "'Cause she liked it," he said after a moment's consideration. He lifted a shoulder in a careless shrug as he levered the potatoes on his plate. "A man can tell when a woman's enjoying a kiss."

"If she was enjoying it so much, then why she did try to break your foot? And why did she slap you just now?" Mary Claire persisted.

Hank just shook his head. "Beats me. Like I said, she was enjoying it just fine, then all of a sudden she does this little twister act and starts swinging and kicking and acting all insulted. If you don't believe me, ask her. If she's honest, she'll tell you the same damn thing."

Mary Claire sank down on her chair, convinced that Hank was telling the truth, at least the part about the slap. The evidence was there right before her, staining his left cheek. She knew that Leighanna had changed since she'd moved to Temptation. She'd seen a new strength in her friend, a confidence that she'd never exhibited while living in Houston. But to physically attack someone? Mary Claire dropped her face in her hands.

Thinking he'd somehow upset her and she was about to cry, Hank nearly choked on a mouthful of potatoes when Mary Claire started laughing.

He dropped his fork to his plate in disgust. "And what, may I ask, is so damn funny?"

Unable to stop laughing, Mary Claire flapped a weak

hand at him. "It's not you. It's Leighanna. I can't believe she had the nerve to really hit you."

Hank rubbed a hand across his cheek, working his jaw to make sure it was still intact. "Trust me. She had the nerve, all right." He dropped his hand and reached for the platter of steak. "Scared her, though," he said, chuckling as he remembered the fear in her eyes. "Once she cooled off enough to realize what she'd done, she was worried that I was going to fire her."

Mary Claire instantly sobered, knowing how much Leighanna needed this job. "Are you?" she asked nervously.

"Don't see why I should," Hank replied as he stabbed his fork into a steak and levered it onto his plate. "She does what work I assign her. Even volunteers for extra." He frowned, glancing Mary Claire's way. "She even volunteered to paint The End of the Road. Is she really that desperate for money?"

Since it was obvious Leighanna hadn't shared her financial problems with Hank, Mary Claire didn't consider it appropriate for her to discuss them with him now. "You'll have to ask Leighanna that question," she replied. "It's not my place to say."

The tables were beautiful, the flickering candles beneath the globes adding just the right touch of ambience that Leighanna had hoped for. She fussed around the tables, smoothing the cloths and straightening the occasional leaning globe...but the kinks of tension Hank's kiss had put in her stomach weren't as easily dealt with.

Sighing, she dragged out a chair and dropped down on it, propping her elbows on the checkered cloth and covering her face with her hands. Hank was right, she thought miserably. She was afraid of him, afraid of what his kisses did to her.

But how could something as simple as a kiss be so devastating? she asked herself for the hundredth time since arriving at the bar.

Because it wasn't simple, came her conscience's reply...and Leighanna had to agree. There had been nothing, not from the first touch of his lips on hers to the last moment when he'd stepped away, that was simple. It had been world shattering. Bone melting. Heart wrenching.

Roger's kisses had never made her feel that way. In comparison Roger's kisses had been teasing, almost playful. Hank's had been anything but. He drew at a primitiveness within her that she hadn't even known existed. Sexual, she thought on a trembling sigh. Purely sexual. His kiss had promised sex, hot and satisfying...and she'd been more than ready to cash in on that promise.

But then he'd stopped, withdrawing from her a little too easily as if the kiss had meant nothing to him, when it had meant everything to her. That, more than the kiss itself, was what had made her slap him. More than he'd angered her, he'd insulted her with his casual disregard for something that affected her so strongly.

She opened her palm, staring at it, able, even now, to feel the sting of the slap.

But I'll take heed of the warning, she remembered him saying. *Next time it'll be you kissing me.*

Leighanna dropped her hands to her lap and squeezed them into a tight ball. Next time? Would there be a next time?

Before she could pursue that thought, a noise came from outside. Knowing it was probably Hank returning to the bar, she rocketed to her feet. In her haste, her chair toppled over backward, crashing to the floor behind her. Through the front windows, she watched as his truck flashed past and disappeared around the corner of the building.

Her heart kicked into a rib-rattling beat. Already yearning for that next time, she placed her hand over her breast to keep her heart from pounding right out of her chest. She forced herself to take long, deep breaths, strengthening her resolve.

There won't be a next time, she told herself firmly. She wouldn't, couldn't let herself get involved with another man.

Especially not one like Hank Braden, who probably notched his bedpost with every new conquest.

Dreading seeing him again so soon, she quickly grabbed the chair and righted it just before the back door slammed shut and Hank appeared in the opening that led to the kitchen.

"I'm gonna take a shower," he called to her. "Can you handle things alone until I get cleaned up?"

If she had expected anger or a cold shoulder directed her way for the slap she'd given him, she would have been disappointed. His expression was free of any sign of condemnation, his tone neutral at the very worst.

Determined to appear as unaffected as he by what had passed between them, Leighanna cinched her fingers tight around the chair's back for support and forced a smile to her lips. "Yes, I'll be fine."

Hank started to turn away, then turned back, bracing a hand on either side of the door frame. A frown furrowed his forehead. "While I was at Mary Claire's eating lunch, I asked her why you were so desperate for money."

Leighanna's fingers tightened on the chair. "What did she tell you?"

"She said I'd have to ask you."

Leighanna's fingers relaxed, but only a little. "Why do you want to know?"

He lifted a shoulder in a shrug. "Just curious."

Turning her back on him, Leighanna kneed the chair back into place under the table. "I have debts to pay off."

Hank snorted. "I swear. You women and your credit cards."

Leighanna whirled to face him. "They aren't *my* debts," she said furiously.

"Then why the hell are you paying them?"

"Because—" She stopped, embarrassed to admit her own naiveté in allowing Roger to sink her so deeply in debt. "Because, in a sense, they are mine," she murmured.

Hank tossed up his hands. "Damnation! They either are, or they aren't. Which is it?"

Leighanna's cheek burned in both anger and humiliation. "They're mine, because they were incurred by my husband."

Hank's eyes widened. *Husband?* It had never occurred to him that Leighanna might have a husband. "You're married?"

She quickly shook her head. "No. Divorced."

Hank almost sighed in relief. He might like women, but he made it a rule to never fool around with another man's wife. "Then why isn't *he* paying the debts?" he asked, still confused.

"Because he won't...or he can't." She waved the explanation away as if it didn't matter. "Either way, I have to repay them or my credit rating is ruined."

Hank studied her, his arms folded across his chest, mentally adding integrity to the growing list of character traits he'd discovered in Leighanna. "So why didn't you stay in Houston? Surely the job market is better there than here?"

There was no way Leighanna would admit to Hank that she'd left Houston on the run because she was so weak that she couldn't say no to Roger. "I needed a change," she replied, somewhat vaguely, hoping he would drop the subject.

"What kind of change?"

Leighanna rolled her eyes in frustration. "A change! You know, new town, new people, new job."

"New husband?"

Leighanna stiffened her spine defensively. "I don't recall mentioning wanting a husband."

"No, but that's what the media's pushing for with all their talk about the man-to-woman ratio here in Temptation. Half the folks that have trooped through here to check out the place are single women looking for a husband. Just figured maybe you were, too."

"I assure you, my reasons for moving to Temptation did *not* include seeking a husband."

Though he doubted her motives for moving to Temptation, Hank gave his shoulder a whatever-you-say shrug. "Do you like it here better than you did Houston?"

Relieved to have his inquisition take a different slant, Leighanna's shoulders relaxed. "Yes, I do."

"Why?"

"Because the pace is slower, the people are friendly and the town has a charm all its own."

Hank chuckled. "Careful. Cody'll be using you for one of his advertisements to lure people to Temptation."

Leighanna smiled in spite of herself. "I seriously doubt my opinion would sway anyone in this direction."

"Maybe. Maybe not." Hank started to turn away again, then turned back. "By the way, the tables look good," he said, and shot her a wink before turning toward his apartment again.

Four

The front door to The End of the Road opened and slammed shut.

Startled by the unexpected noise, Leighanna glanced up and was startled even more to see Mrs. Martin standing just inside the entrance, her hands fisted on her wide hips. In the week Leighanna had worked at the bar, Mrs. Martin was the first female of Temptation's population to pass the threshold.

"Had to see it for myself to believe it!" Mrs. Martin exclaimed as she gaped openly at the covered tables. "But dang if you didn't go and put cloths on the table, just like you said you were going to do!"

Leighanna smiled as she rounded the bar to greet Mrs. Martin, pleased by the woman's praise as much as she was by her presence there. "Lovely, aren't they?"

Mrs. Martin gave a curt nod as she shuffled into the room. "They're sure that." She dragged a chair from beneath a table near the bar and settled her wide girth onto its seat. "What have you got other than beer to wet a person's throat?" she asked brusquely.

"Soft drinks. Tea. What would you like?"

"A soda will do, doesn't matter what flavor, just so it's wet and cold." She pulled a wrinkled handkerchief from her dress's pocket and mopped her sweaty brow. "Where's that scoundrel Hank?" she asked as she leaned to poke a gnarled finger at the centerpieces Leighanna had made.

Leighanna bit back a smile at the woman's impertinence. "He's in his apartment."

"Tell that good-for-nothing so-and-so that he's got himself a customer out here."

Not sure whether Hank had had the time to shower and dress, Leighanna hesitated.

"Well? What are you waiting for?" Mrs. Martin huffed impatiently. "Go and get him!"

With a sigh Leighanna turned to do her bidding, but before she took a step in that direction, Hank strode from the kitchen, bare from the waist up and rubbing a towel over his wet hair. The sight of that bare chest had Leighanna reeling.

He stopped short when he saw Mrs. Martin sitting at the table. His lips curved into a welcoming smile as he dropped the towel around his neck. "Well if it isn't the queen of Main Street!" he exclaimed and headed straight for her table. Catching her hand, he pulled her up, then wrapped his arms around her in a bear hug and swung her off her feet, dancing her in a fast dizzying circle.

Leighanna could do nothing but stare.

"Unhand me, you beast," Mrs. Martin sputtered as she struggled to tug his arms from around her waist. Hank settled her on her feet and dipped his head to give her a smack full on the lips. The woman's face reddened, but Leighanna thought she caught a glint of pleasure in the old woman's eyes as she tussled her dress back in place over her hips.

"You'll never change," Mrs. Martin muttered disagreeably. "Always hustlin' a woman, no matter what her age."

Hank just grinned that woman-killing grin of his and angled the chair and held it so that Mrs. Martin could sit back down. He surprised Leighanna by pulling out another chair, and taking a seat beside her.

"And what brings you to The End of the Road?" he asked, teasing her with a smile.

"Humph! Had to see for myself what all changes were going on over here. Couldn't believe it when Leighanna came in and bought that cloth for the tables." She smoothed an age-freckled hand across the checkered cloth. "Looks real nice," she added, giving a nod of approval. "Though I'm sure Jedidiah is turning over in his grave."

Jedidiah? Unable to stem her curiosity, Leighanna took a step toward them. "Who's Jedidiah?"

Mrs. Martin twisted her head around to frown at Leighanna as if she thought Leighanna should have known the man. "He ran this place right up until his death. God rest his soul," she murmured, quickly crossing herself. Frowning again, she leaned back in her chair and folded her hands in her lap. "He was meaner than sin, but always had a soft spot for Hank, here," she added, pursing her lips at him and appraising him in a skeptical way. "God knows why. Jedidiah refused to sell the place to anybody but him, even though there were others who'd have gladly paid a bigger price."

"I'm sure that it was my charm and keen business sense that attracted him," Hank returned, grinning.

"Pshaw! You don't have a lick of charm, except for the ladies, and the only good business sense you've ever shown was in hiring Leighanna."

Leighanna winced at the praise, remembering well Hank's irritation over all the attention the clean windows had drawn. She was sure that Mrs. Martin's comments would anger him just as much. But when Hank glanced Leighanna's way, his gaze was more assessing than judgmental, and it was all she could do to keep her mouth from dropping open.

Mrs. Martin either didn't see the exchange or chose to ignore it. "Personally," she continued, "I've always wondered if Jedidiah might have done it to alleviate his guilt because he thought he was the one who fathered you." She narrowed her eyes, peering at Hank intently. "You've got his eyes, and that's a fact."

Leighanna saw Hank's face redden and a vein at his temple begin to pulse. Knowing that he probably wasn't enjoying having his illegitimacy discussed in front of her, she turned away and headed for the bar to fill Mrs. Martin's request for a soda. But their voices carried, and Leighanna couldn't help but hear the rest of their conversation.

"My eyes are my own," Hank muttered defensively. "And you know as well as I do that any one of a hundred or more men could have fathered me."

"Can't argue that." Mrs. Martin's ample breasts rose and fell on a heavyhearted sigh. "Just seems a shame that no one stepped up and claimed you as their own, especially after your mother passed on. Everybody needs family."

Hank shoved back his chair and stood. "Not me," he

said, catching the towel's ends in his hands. "I get along just fine on my own." In spite of the anger that still stained his cheeks, he dipped his head and pressed a kiss on Mrs. Martin's cheek, then gave her shoulder an affectionate pat. "But thanks for the concern."

Flustered, she waved him away. "Go get yourself some clothes on before I call Cody and have him arrest you for indecent exposure."

Behind the bar, Leighanna let out a shuddery sigh as she watched Hank stroll past her and disappear into the kitchen once again. She waited for the sound of his apartment door at the back opening and closing before picking up Mrs. Martin's soda and rounding the bar.

Though her heart was breaking at the false bravado she'd detected in Hank's voice when he'd claimed he got along just fine without family, she forced a smile to her face as she set the glass in front of Mrs. Martin. "Here you go," she said pleasantly. "Would you like anything else?"

Mrs. Martin gave the chair Hank had just vacated a nod. "A little company's all," she replied.

Leighanna sank down on the chair, instantly aware of the heat it still held from Hank's body.

Mrs. Martin picked up her drink and eyed Leighanna over its rim. "Are you sleeping with him yet?" she asked bluntly.

Leighanna's mouth dropped open in surprise. "I beg your pardon?"

"I said, are you sleeping with him yet? You've been working here, what, a week?"

"Yes," Leighanna whispered, then quickly corrected any misconceptions Mrs. Martin might entertain by adding, "I mean that, yes, I've been working here a week."

"Most women would have fallen for his charm by then."

"I'm not most women."

Mrs. Martin tilted her head, frowning as she studied Leighanna's face. "No," she said slowly. "I can see that you're not. But you're not immune to him, either," she added. "I can see that, as well."

Leighanna felt color rise up her neck to stain her cheeks.

Mrs. Martin nodded sagely. "I figured as much." She surprised Leighanna by chuckling. "Mark my word. He'll have you in his bed 'fore the month's up." She chuckled again, wagging her head. "You oughta sell tickets. Watching your fall would be well worth the price, no matter what the cost."

Leighanna parked in front of the hardware store and stepped from her car, dabbing at the perspiration on her forehead. She was going to have to get that air conditioner repaired and soon, she told herself. Otherwise, she'd melt before the summer was over.

"Hey, Leighanna! How you doin'?"

Leighanna glanced up to see Cody strolling down the sidewalk toward her. She waved a greeting. A frequent customer at The End of the Road, Cody had endeared himself to her the day he'd commented on the clean windows. "Fine, thanks," she replied, smiling. "How about you?"

"Can't complain. Though we could stand a little rain. Would cool things down a bit." He stopped and waited for her to climb the two steps that led from the street to the hardware store. "What brings you to town?"

"Supplies. I'm doing some painting at The End of the Road tomorrow."

"Really?" Cody tossed a friendly arm across her shoulders and walked with her into the store. "That's quite a job to take on in this heat."

"I'm planning on getting an early start."

With a nod at the store's owner, Cody trailed Leighanna down the aisle. "How are you and Hank getting along?"

Leighanna tensed at the mention of Hank, remembering Mrs. Martin's prediction that before the month ended she'd be in his bed. She wondered if everyone in town thought she was sleeping with Hank.

She forced her shoulders to relax. "Fine." She reached for a sample card of paint colors and pretended to study it. "He does his work, I do mine."

Cody nodded his head. "Sounds like a fair deal." He hooked an arm along the edge of an upper shelf. "Is painting part of your job description as a waitress?"

Leighanna stuck the card back in the rack and chose another. "No. This is in addition to my normal duties. I need the money."

"Who doesn't?" Cody dipped his head and thoughtfully rubbed a finger beneath his nose. "If you're interested in making a little more, you might talk to Mayor Acres. He's looking for someone to head up a committee to plan a little celebration he's putting on at the end of the month."

The prospect of increasing her income making her instantly alert, Leighanna turned to him. "Really?"

Cody nodded his head. "Yep. He's hoping to fill the town's coffers from all the media attention that's come Temptation's way." He lifted his shoulder in a shrug. "The job probably won't pay much, but if you're interested, I could put a bug in Acres's ear for you."

She laid a hand on his arm, her eyes bright with excitement. "Would you? Oh, Cody, I'd be grateful."

"No trouble," he mumbled, obviously embarrassed by her gratitude.

Her mind already racing, Leighanna caught her lower lip between her teeth. "My shift at The End of the Road is from five until closing time, but I suppose I can work around that. If it's all right with Mayor Acres, I could work for him in the morning and in the early afternoon, then for Hank at night."

"I'm sure Acres would agree to that."

"Oh, Cody," she said, unable to contain her excitement. "I really appreciate your telling me about this job."

Cody just shook his head and chuckled. "You might not be so grateful after you've worked with Acres for a while. He can be cantankerous at times. His moods swing faster than the price of grain."

Leighanna arched a brow, thinking of her current employer and his wild mood swings. "He couldn't be any worse than Hank Braden."

By seven a.m. Sunday morning, the sun was already making its presence known. Its rays reflected off the tin roof of The End of the Road and heat radiated from its surface, turning the tin the color of polished silver. Having already worked nearly an hour gathering and setting up her supplies, Leighanna paused at the side of the building, already bone tired, and rested a shoulder against the rough stone.

It had been almost two when she'd arrived home from work the night before, but it was well after four before she'd finally drifted off to sleep. And it was all Hank's fault, she thought on a weary sigh. Ever since that afternoon at Mary Claire's when he'd kissed her, he had haunted her sleep. And he was messing with her mind. She just knew he was. For some unknown reason, he was being nicer to her, even helping her with the duties that he'd originally assigned to her. The night before he had even insisted on mopping the floor while she counted the night's proceeds. And why? she asked herself.

The why behind his sudden change of nature didn't matter, she told herself. She had more important things to concern herself with. And painting Hank's building was at the top of the list. With the prospect of a new job on the horizon, she wanted to have the painting completed so she would be free to take advantage of Mayor Acres's job if he offered it to her. Still, it took all her willpower to step from the shade created by the building and out into the bright sunlight.

After adjusting the six-foot metal ladder she'd found in the shed in front of the bar's entrance, she stooped and turned on the portable radio she'd brought along to keep her company. Switching the station to one that played rhythm and blues, she cranked up the volume, then turned to the makeshift table where she'd set up her supplies. Choosing a pad of steel wool, she moved her hips in rhythm with Bonnie Raitt's voice as she attacked the peeling varnish on the front door. Working with the grain, just as her father had taught her years ago, she scrubbed, chipping away at the old varnish and baring the wood beneath.

Birds sang in a nearby tree, and Leighanna added her voice to theirs, singing lustily right along with Bonnie Raitt. The words were familiar, the beat fast, pumping up the speed of Leighanna's hand as she pushed the stiff wool up and down over the wood.

Unaware of anything but the pulsing sound of the music around her and the door beneath her hand, Leighanna suddenly found herself flat on her face when the door was jerked open from the inside.

"What in the hell are you trying to do? Wake the dead?"

Warily, she lifted her head a fraction to find a pair of bare feet planted an inch from her nose. Slowly she lifted her gaze higher, skimming up denim-clad legs, hesitating only slightly at the three buttons left open at the jean's fly, but coming to a shocking halt when her gaze hit on the bare skin created by the jeans' opening. A little higher and muscled pecs, tensed in anger, swelled beneath a fur of thick black hair. Swallowing hard, she forced her gaze higher until she stared unblinkingly into the face of Hank Braden.

His hair still tousled from sleep, he towered over her, his hands on his hips, while a muscle twitched dangerously on his jaw.

Slowly pushing herself to her feet, she bent to dust off her knees. "I'm sorry. It didn't occur to me that you would still be asleep or I would have—" She winced when her fingers hit a raw spot on her knee. Bending at the waist, she saw that blood oozed from the scrape.

"Now look what you've done," she said, fighting back tears. "You've bloodied my knee."

"*I've* bloodied your knee! You're the one who fell!"

She snapped up her head to glare at him. "I wouldn't have if you hadn't opened the door so unexpectedly." Tucking her chin, she examined the scrape.

Hank dipped his head over hers to look, as well. "Ah, hell. It's just a little scratch," he muttered.

"It's bleeding, isn't it?" she cried indignantly.

Cursing under his breath, Hank grabbed her by the wrist and wheeled, dragging her behind him.

"What do you think you're doing?" she cried as she stumbled after him.

"I'm gonna doctor that knee before you develop blood poisoning and the damn thing rots off."

With his hand cinched tightly around her wrist, Leigh-anna was forced to run to keep up with him. He didn't stop until he reached his apartment at the rear of the bar. At the door, he slowed only long enough to push her through the doorway ahead of him. "Take a seat there on the bed while I grab my first aid kit from the bathroom."

Stunned, Leighanna watched him disappear behind a door. *Sit on his bed?* Slowly she turned to stare at the item in question. A tangle of sheets and blankets covered the old iron bed, a heady reminder that Hank had just climbed from it. She could almost see him there, naked, stretched across its length, and wondered what it would be like to lie there with him. With a moan of frustration at her lustful thoughts, she tore her gaze away and looked for a less intimate place to sit...but discovered there wasn't one.

The apartment consisted of only one room, with a small kitchen tucked into one corner. A dresser lined the wall to her left. On its dusty surface sat a television, angled for easy viewing from the bed positioned opposite it.

Beside the bed was a small nightstand which held a dilapidated lamp and a plate smeared with dried ketchup. It seemed the bed was the center of activity, used for everything from sleeping, to eating, to relaxing while watching the tube. A shiver shook her shoulders as she wondered what else it was used for.

Before she could ponder this further, Hank stepped from the bathroom, carrying a small box and a washcloth dripping water. With a huff of impatience that she hadn't followed his instructions, he gave her a shove that sent her sprawling across the mattress.

"Prop your knee up," he ordered as he tossed the box onto the bed beside her.

Pushing herself to her elbows, Leighanna glared at him, but hooked a foot on the bed rail, presenting her knee, anxious to get this over with and out of his apartment. He stooped over her, dabbing the wet cloth at the scrape. Wincing, Leighanna jerked away. He immediately stopped and glanced up at her. "Did that hurt?"

"A little," she murmured reluctantly.

Grunting, he squatted down in front of her and reapplied the cloth, but gentler this time. With him hunkered down in front of her, Leighanna found herself confronted with an unrestricted view of his bare chest. The muscled pecs tightened and swelled with each stroke of his hand. She remembered well the feel of that chest pressed against her, but the sight of it naked was almost more than she could bear. Her breath grew shorter and shorter until she had to force herself to look away, to focus instead on his hands...though doing so didn't offer much relief.

The fingers that held the cloth were thick, the palms wide and the skin beneath the hair that dusted the back of his hand tanned a golden brown. The hands were those of a working man, callused and strong, yet his touch was painfully gentle, reminding her of other times when he'd touched her. Now, like then, heat surged through her body at the contact, and she found herself aching for an even more intimate touch.

At that moment he glanced up at her, but Leighanna's gaze never made it any higher than his lips.

Next time, it'll be you kissing me...

She caught her bottom lip between her teeth as his words came back to haunt her, wishing with all her heart that he'd ignore her warning, as he had before, and try to kiss her again. She knew without a doubt that this time she would let him. She might even beg him. She raised her gaze higher.

"I'm gonna—" Hank stopped when her eyes met his, and he rocked back on his heels, a grin chipping at the corner of his mouth. "You're thinking about that kiss, aren't you?"

Leighanna stiffened, mortified that he could read her thoughts so easily. "Don't be ridiculous!"

Hank just chuckled. "Oh, you're thinking about it, all right." He tucked his tongue in the corner of his mouth as he eyed her, then nodded knowingly. "And you're wondering if it was as good as you remember it." When her face reddened, he chuckled again. "Trust me, sweetheart," he said with a wink. "It was."

Leighanna sucked in an outraged breath. "You are undoubtedly the most egotistical man I've ever met."

Hank just shrugged. "Maybe. But it takes two to make a kiss memorable. And believe me, sweetheart, I haven't forgotten that kiss, either."

Leighanna's eyes widened in surprise. "You haven't?"

"Well, hell no." His gaze took on a considering look. "But maybe that's because we've never really finished a kiss."

She swallowed hard, unable to fathom what the end of a kiss meant to Hank. "We haven't?"

"Not in my book." He continued to stare at her, his eyes warming and darkening in that look that both frightened and aroused her. "Maybe we should have another go at it. Just to see if what we experienced was as good as we remember it.''

Leighanna knotted her fingers in the tangle of bedcovers at her sides, knowing full well that in agreeing to his suggestion she was playing with fire. "I suppose we could do that," she said nervously.

Hank rocked forward until his feet were flat on the floor again. Drawing her hitched leg from the bed rail, he guided both her legs around him, then slowly dropped to his knees until he knelt in the V he'd created with her legs.

Holding her legs snug against his hips, he leaned forward, but stopped just shy of her lips. He drew away, eyeing her suspiciously. "You're not going to slap me again, now are you?"

She shook her head, her eyes riveted on his mouth. "No." She wet her lips, already thinking of the feel of that sensuous mouth on hers. "No," she repeated. "I won't slap you."

Satisfied, he nodded and leaned toward her again. She closed her eyes, drifting to meet him…and nearly tumbled into his lap when he jerked away from her again. "What about kicking or stomping?" he asked, frowning. "You planning on doing anything like that?"

Not sure now whether she wanted to kiss him or kill him, Leighanna clapped her hands against the sides of his face. Digging her fingers into his cheeks, she glared down at him. "For God's sake, will you *please* just kiss me and get it over with?"

Chuckling, Hank scooted closer. "Yes, ma'am. I surely will. But as to getting it over with, now I can't make any promises about that." Slowly, he lifted his face and closed his mouth over hers. Catching her lower lip between his, he drew it deep into his mouth, suckling gently.

Shivers chased down Leighanna's spine while arrows of need shot straight to her feminine core. This is what had haunted her, she thought weakly as his tongue slipped into her mouth. This is what had kept her awake night after night, ruining her sleep. This is what drove her crazy each time he brushed against her when they worked side by side at the bar.

On a low moan of surrender, she looped her hands around his neck and slid bonelessly from the bed, landing with a soft plop against his thighs while her breasts melted against his chest. Giving herself up to the tastes and the textures, to the raw level of need that pulled at her, she moved her hips in rhythm with the movements of his lips on hers.

And Hank was sure he would die.

The feel of her, the pressure of her body rubbing against his, that seductive feminine scent she'd dabbed in all the right spots.... He'd never been to heaven, didn't have a prayer of ever crossing through those pearly gates, but he knew this had to be what heaven must be like and about as close to the place as a man like him could get. With her knees squeezed around him, those small, firm breasts of hers pressing hard against his chest, that tongue of hers playing a game of tag with his in her mouth...well, it was more than he'd bargained for and definitely more of a temptation than he was willing to let pass.

Loosening his hold on her legs, he dragged his hands upward, running them up the tautened muscles of her thighs to cup her denim-clad buttocks. He paused there a moment, enjoying the feel of her muscles tightening beneath his hands before he slipped his hands higher to slide under the hem of her T-shirt.

Silk and sandpaper, he thought as his callused hands skimmed her smooth back. Yet another contrast between them to explore. But later, he told himself. At the moment he had only one thing on his mind, and that was to simply give and take a little pleasure.

Drawing his hands slowly away from her spine, he shaped them around her sides, noting again the delicacy of her small frame and the fullness of her small, unencumbered breasts. His thumb grazed a nipple, and he felt the purr of a moan vibrate against his lips. His or hers? he wondered fleetingly before he took her breasts fully into his hands. This time he recognized the moan that vibrated between them as his own. He remembered well teasing her about what little God had blessed her with and telling her that some men liked women with small breasts...he just wasn't one of them. But with the weight of her breasts in his hands, with her turgid nipples stabbing at his palm, he knew that he'd been wrong.

And he knew he had to taste them.

But would she let him? he wondered. If something as innocent as a kiss had earned him a foot stomping and a face slapping, what would she do if he dared to bare her breasts? He steeled himself for whatever punishment she inflicted, knowing it would be well worth the pain.

In an action smoothed by years of practice, he had her T-shirt over her head and his mouth pressed over hers once again to smother any protest...but to his surprise, none was forthcoming. Her only response was a low whimper that originated low in her throat and slowly died there as she tightened her arms around him, pressing her naked breasts against his chest.

And now it was just skin against skin. The desire to

be closer still was overpowering. Cupping her buttocks in his hands, he stood, lifting her with him. Instinctively she wrapped her legs around his waist as he dug a knee into the mattress. He laid her down on his bed, then followed, covering her body with his. Unable to stand the temptation any longer, he shifted, tearing his mouth from hers and closing it over a breast.

With a sharp cry of pleasure, Leighanna arched, thrusting herself hard against him. She'd never felt so utterly out of control before, so detached from herself. Was this like death? she wondered. If so, she welcomed it with open arms. The sensations that ripped through her robbed her of air and numbed her to everything but the feel of that hot, clever mouth against her breast. His teeth nipped, his lips soothed, his tongue laved a path from one breast to the other…and left the first aching for more. Never in her life had she throbbed like this. Never had she felt this overpowering need for a man's touch. She wanted him to do more than kiss her, she wanted, with a fervency she'd never experienced in her life, for him to make love to her.

The idea that she would even consider such a thing pushed ice through her veins. She had to stop him, she thought wildly, before she totally lost control.

She caught his face in her hands and forced his mouth back to hers. But instead of stopping him, her actions seemed to incite him even more. With a growl, he shifted again, dragging his body up the length of hers, and she nearly wept at the length of hardened maleness that pressed against her femininity. It took every fiber of will she possessed, but she pressed her hands more firmly against his cheeks and tore her mouth from his.

With her chest heaving with each drawn breath, she met his gaze. Their eyes seemed to weld together in the heat that burned between them. She saw the passion in his brown eyes, that wild unsatisfied yearning, and knew it must be mirrored in her own. It would be so easy, she thought with a stab of regret, to give in to that passion and let it carry them on. But she couldn't. She knew she couldn't. She didn't trust herself when it came to dealing with men, especially a man like Hank Braden.

Struggling to remain calm, she nervously wet her lips. "I think we're finished," she said, but was unable to keep the telltale tremble from her voice. "I need to get back to work."

For a moment he continued to stare at her, then slowly his lips curved into a smile. "Are you sure?"

Though returning to work wasn't at all what she wanted to do, she gave her chin a quick jerk. "Yes. I'm sure."

"All right then." He shifted his weight until he was stretched out beside her.

With his body no longer shielding her nakedness, Leighanna instinctively tried to cover herself, but Hank placed an arm between hers, preventing her. "We'll have none of that."

Holding her in place with nothing but the strength in his gaze, he gently forced her arms down to her sides and rested his arm across her abdomen. His hand molded the gentle curve of her waist. He lowered his face to hers and Leighanna stiffened, fearing that he was going to kiss her again and not at all certain she would have the strength to stop him this time.

"Before you go, sweetheart," he said, his breath feathering at her lips. "You need to understand one thing. We haven't even come close to finishing that kiss."

Five

A week later, Leighanna sat at Mary Claire's kitchen table with her chin cradled in her palm, staring at the oak tree outside the kitchen window, her thoughts as fleeting as the summer breeze that sent the leaves on the old oak dancing. Her checkbook, a stack of bills and a legal pad with a carefully planned budget were spread on the table in front of her. With the money Hank had paid her for painting The End of the Road, she had decisions to make...which bill to pay first.

But Leighanna couldn't concentrate on the task at hand. Hank refused to let her. He was there, if only in her mind, pushing himself to the forefront of her thoughts and making it all but impossible to focus on anything but him.

Oddly enough, it wasn't the seductive power of his kisses that plagued her, though she had spent some time dwelling on that. It was simply...him. In her mind she kept seeing again his apartment, that old iron bed with its tangle of covers, that plate sitting on the nightstand with dried ketchup smeared across its surface. Along with the vision came the memory of what Mrs. Martin had unwittingly revealed about his past. No roots. No family.

And Leighanna's heart ached for him. For the child he'd been, without a father or a mother to look out for him, without a place to call home. And for the man he'd become, who tried to pretend that he didn't need any of those things.

But he did. She knew he did. At the time she might have been momentarily blinded to everything but the passion he drew from her, but on reflection she remembered the gentleness of his touch, the sighs of contentment when he'd held her tight in his arms. She remembered, too, the fondness he'd shown Mrs. Martin, a woman more than twice his age, a woman who cared for him like a mother would.

Because Leighanna understood those needs, that same yearning for love and affection that she herself craved, she recognized them in Hank.

But there was a difference between Hank and herself. Leighanna had known a mother's love, the security in having a home, even if the address *had* kept changing over the years. She wanted only to duplicate those things, improve on what she'd experienced as a child. She wanted to love someone, and to have that someone love her in return. Beyond that, she wanted a home, a spot of security and permanency that she could call her own. And though she'd married once and failed to see that dream fulfilled, she still believed she would one day live it.

In comparison, Hank sought fulfillment for those same needs in an unending line of willing women, much like his mother had in the succession of men she'd bedded.

A part of Leighanna, a secret part that she dared not examine too closely, wanted to give him what he needed. She wanted to love him and nurture him, to fill the voids in his life, to—

"What are you daydreaming about?"

Leighanna jumped at the sound of Mary Claire's voice and guiltily began to shuffle through the stack of bills, trying to appear busy. "Nothing. Just paying bills."

Mary Claire set a basket of laundry on the opposite end of the table and plucked out a towel to fold, biting back a smile. "Never knew a bill could bring such a dreamy look to a woman's eye."

Leighanna's face warmed. "The truth is," she admitted reluctantly. "I was thinking about Hank."

Mary Claire's fingers stilled on the towel, and she glanced Leighanna's way. "Hank?"

Leighanna's forehead puckered into a thoughtful frown. "Did you know that he hasn't a clue as to who fathered him?"

"No," Mary Claire murmured hesitantly. "Though I have heard rumors that his mother...well, that his mother was rather loose."

Leighanna snorted. "Loose is putting it mildly. According to Mrs. Martin, Hank all but raised himself. To quote her, 'Hank's mother was so busy slipping out of one bed and into another that half the time she'd even forget to take him with her when she made the shift.'"

Not having heard this before, Mary Claire set the folded towel aside and thoughtfully picked up another, her mother's heart breaking for the child Hank had once been. "Poor little fellow. He must have been pretty tough to have survived unscathed."

"I don't think he did."

Mary Claire dropped the towel she was folding to look at Leighanna in confusion. "What?"

"Think about Hank's reputation. If everything that is rumored about him is true, he is obviously trying to fill the voids in his life with all his flirting and with all the women he's supposedly bedded. Considering his past and his mother's loose ways, that's the only way that he would know how."

Mary Claire snatched the towel she'd dropped from the basket and pursed her lips as she began to fold it. "Leighanna," she warned. "Don't even think it."

"Think what?" Leighanna asked in surprise.

"That Hank Braden is some kind of wounded bird that you can adopt and heal."

Insulted, Leighanna tilted up her chin. "I wasn't thinking of adopting him."

"Well, what *are* you thinking?" Before Leighanna could answer, Mary Claire dropped down in the chair opposite her and gathered her friend's hands in hers. "I know you, Leighanna," she said gently. "Probably better than you know yourself. You have the softest heart in the world and it would be just like you to think that you could take Hank under your wing and make up to him for all the neglect he's experienced in his life."

"Don't be ridiculous," Leighanna sputtered defensively and tried to pull her hands away. But Mary Claire refused to let her go, forcing Leighanna to meet her gaze.

"You'll only get hurt, Leighanna," she murmured. "And I don't want to see that happen."

"For heaven's sake!" Leighanna cried. "You're talking as if I was planning on marrying him!" She tugged her hands free of Mary Claire's and sat back in her chair with a huff. "I just thought that I should be nicer to him, more understanding. In fact, if it's all right with you, I'd like to invite him to have lunch with us on Sunday."

By Thursday night, Leighanna was beginning to panic. She'd been trying all week to find just the right moment to offer the invitation to Hank, but business at the bar had been crazy, at best.

The new decor had set up a furor around town and it seemed like everyone in the county was determined to drop in and see for themselves all the changes The End of the Road had undergone. Naturally, that meant more work for Leighanna and Hank, which kept them hustling all evening, with not a second to themselves so that she could invite him as she'd planned.

But she was determined that tonight before she went home, she would offer the invitation. Her arms elbow-deep in dishwater, Leighanna racked her brain, trying to think of an opening, some casual way to invite Hank to lunch at Mary Claire's without it sounding like a date, or worse, a come-on. Unfortunately, nothing came to mind.

"Heard Mayor Acres hired you to head up the committee that's throwing that bash on Labor Day weekend."

Leighanna glanced over at Hank, who was working about ten steps away, wiping down the grill, and silently cursed herself for not already telling him about the job herself. She'd been in such a stew all evening about the lunch invitation, the new job had totally slipped her mind. "Yes, he did," she said, hoping to hide her guilt behind a smile. "In fact, I start Monday. But don't worry," she assured him as she dipped the last plate into the rinse water, then laid it on the drain with the others to dry.

"The hours I work for him won't conflict with my hours here."

Hank merely grunted and picked up a cloth. He plucked a plate from the drain and began to dry. "Don't I pay you enough?"

Hearing the edge in his voice, Leighanna rested her hands on the lip of the sink and turned to look at him. "Well, of course you do. I just—"

"Need the money," he finished for her.

"Yes, I do," she replied firmly.

Hank merely shook his head as he set the plate aside and selected another to dry. "Sweetheart, you're gonna work yourself into an early grave."

Leighanna bit back a smile, knowing she had been right about Hank. There was a soft spot buried beneath that flirtatious, skirt-chasing man's skin. "A little hard work never killed anyone," she said lightly. "Besides, the job will only last until Labor Day."

Hank focused his gaze on the plate he was drying and frowned. "I suppose I could give you a raise."

Leighanna arched her brows, surprised by the offer. "A raise would be appreciated, I assure you, but I certainly don't expect one. Heavens!" she said, laughing. "I've worked here less than a month!"

"Doesn't matter how long you've been here," he argued. "The fact is, you've earned it."

Touched by his concern, Leighanna laid a hand on his arm. "Thank you. But if you're thinking a raise will discourage me from accepting the job from Mayor Acres, it won't," she warned him. "The extra money I'll make will help me pay off my debts that much sooner." She sighed softly as he continued to frown, then she turned back to the sink and pulled out the plug, wondering if this might be the very opening she needed. "Would you like to come to Mary Claire's for lunch on Sunday?"

Hank snapped up his head, his hands stilling on the half-dried plate. "Lunch?"

Leighanna turned to him and couldn't help but smile at his startled expression. Obviously he didn't receive invitations for Sunday lunch very often. "Yes, lunch," she repeated. "Mary Claire always serves a huge meal at noon on Sundays."

"Well, I suppose I could," he murmured uncertainly. "Though I promised Harley I'd help him unload some bulls he's hauling in from a sale."

"I'm sure that won't be a problem since Harley is planning to be there, too." Leighanna took the plate from him and finished drying it. "Plan to be there by noon. And come hungry. Mary Claire always cooks enough to feed a small army."

"Uh-oh," Mary Claire murmured.

Leighanna stepped to her friend's side and peered through the kitchen window above the sink to follow the line of Mary Claire's gaze. In the backyard, Hank lay on the grass beneath the old oak tree, his arms folded across his chest, his eyes closed, obviously enjoying a nap after the big lunch he'd just consumed. In the pasture beyond, she could see Harley walking the fence, checking for breaks.

"Uh-oh, what?" Leighanna asked, not seeing anything to be concerned about.

Mary Claire lifted a hand and pointed to the side of the yard where her children, Stephie and Jimmy, were tiptoeing toward Hank with mischief in their eyes. "Hank's about to be attacked," Mary Claire said, chuckling softly.

Knowing from past experience how disagreeable Hank could be when he was awakened, Leighanna lunged for the back door…but she was too late. Stephie and Jimmy had already pounced, landing on Hank's chest, and were squealing and laughing as they dug their fingers into his ribs, tickling him.

With a roar, Hank bucked, catching both kids around the waist, and flipped them over, turning their backs to the ground and kneeling over them with his knees squeezed at their waists.

Sure that he meant them harm, Leighanna cleared the porch steps in one jump and was racing across the yard to rescue the children from his anger.

"You think you're pretty smart, don't you?" she heard him say in a threatening voice as she ran. "Well, you're not as smart as me."

She ran faster, her heart pounding against her ribs as he continued to hold them prisoner.

"Don't! Don't!" Stephie and Jimmy screamed, laughing hysterically. Shocked by the children's laughter, Leighanna stumbled to a stop behind Hank. She was even more shocked when Hank joined in.

"Say uncle," he teased, while his fingers played their rib cages like he would a piano.

"No," they screamed in unison as they twisted and turned, screeching and laughing as they tried to escape his hold on them.

"Better say uncle," he repeated, chuckling. "Or the tickle monster's going to get you."

"Never!" Jimmy yelled, then collapsed into a fit of giggles as Hank turned his fingers full force on him.

Leighanna folded her arms across her breasts, shaking her head and chuckling softly at this new glimpse of Hank's personality. She'd never seen him act like a child before. The sight softened her heart toward him a little bit more.

Spying Leighanna, Stephie cried, "Leighanna! Help us!"

Hank's fingers stilled, and he glanced over his shoulder to find Leighanna standing behind him...and that was all the diversion the children needed. They wriggled from beneath him and pounced again, wrestling Hank to the ground.

Leighanna felt a hand snake around her ankle and a yank, and before she knew what was happening, she was tumbling to land on top of them with a surprised yelp.

"Get her, kids!" Hank yelled, and suddenly it was Leighanna who was on the bottom and two sets of small hands and a set of decidedly larger and stronger ones were tickling at her ribs.

"Say uncle," Stephie demanded, obviously delighted with this new twist to their game.

"Stop! Please!" Leighanna begged, as she swatted futilely at their hands.

"You gotta say uncle first," Hank warned, grinning as he found a particularly vulnerable spot.

"Uncle, my foot," Mary Claire chided, hauling her children away from the pile. "I swear Hank Braden, you are as bad as the kids," she huffed. "Now get off Leighanna before you break her in half."

His hands stopped tickling but Hank didn't budge an inch. He gazed down at Leighanna, grinning like a fool. Though his eyes were set on Leighanna's, his words were directed to Mary Claire and her children. "She's gotta say uncle first. Right, kids?"

"Right!" Stephie and Jimmy yelled in unison. Rolling her eyes, Mary Claire turned and dragged them to the house.

Leighanna watched them leave in growing panic. Swallowing hard, she turned her gaze to Hank's. She could tell by the look in his eyes that this was a whole new game, and she wasn't at all sure she knew the rules. "Are you going to let me up?" she asked uncertainly.

Hank's knees tightened around her and his fingers found that vulnerable spot again, the one just below the fullness of her breast...but he didn't tickle this time. He stroked his thumb seductively down three ribs and back up. "Not until you say uncle."

Leighanna's eyes widened as she recognized that dark warmth that came into his eyes. She'd tried so hard throughout the meal to keep her distance from him, to make this invitation to lunch as platonic as she'd sworn to Mary Claire it was. And now he was going to kiss her again!

"Uncle!" she blurted out. "Uncle!"

"Coward," he murmured and lowered his face to hers.

Knowing how susceptible she was to his persuasive charm, Leighanna twisted her face away and bucked, trying to get out from beneath him. "I'm not a coward," she grated out.

"Sure you are. You're afraid I'm gonna kiss you again."

She stilled instantly and looked up at him. "I'm not afraid," she lied. "I just want up."

"So get up, then," he teased.

She frowned up at him. "I can't. You're on top of me."

He shrugged a shoulder. "We could shift, and you could be on top, if you like."

"Very funny, Braden," she said dryly.

"I'm not trying to be funny, just trying to get a little kiss."

Leighanna snorted. "A little kiss," she repeated in disgust. "You don't even know the meaning of the term."

Hank just grinned. "Sure I do." Before she could argue further, his mouth was on hers, his lips brushing hers in the sweetest, most chaste way...and she closed her eyes on a defeated sigh, giving herself up to the feel of him, the taste of him. Then, to her disappointment and amazement, Hank was pushing himself up and off her. She opened her eyes to see him standing over her. The kiss had lasted only seconds, but the effects on her system lingered.

He stooped and held out a hand, grinning. "See?" he told her as he hauled her to her feet. He slung a companionable arm around her shoulder and turned her toward the house. "I told you I knew what a little kiss was."

A long, gooseneck cattle trailer was backed up to the corral at Harley's ranch. Inside, three bulls pawed and shifted, sending the trailer rocking beneath them as they rammed their horned heads against the steel bars that confined them, looking for a way of escape.

Standing alongside Mary Claire at a safe distance from the trailer, Leighanna fought back a shudder.

"They look mean," she whispered under her breath.

"They are mean," Mary Claire whispered in return as she nervously watched Harley move to the trailer's rear door. She raised her voice to yell a warning to Stephie and Jimmy who were playing King of the Mountain on a stack of hay piled high near the barn door. "You kids stay right where you are until the bulls are unloaded, you hear me?"

"We will, Mom," they called in unison.

With their eyes riveted on the men, Mary Claire and

Leighanna watched as Hank swung open one of the trailer's rear doors and Harley swung open the other and quickly moved behind it. A Brahma bull, his eyes wild from the forced confinement, lowered his head and charged for the opening, catching his horn between the door's iron rails on Harley's side and tossing it back. Before Harley could react, the door slammed into him and sent him flying, his arms striking at the air. He landed flat on his back with a grunt of pain, while dust churned around him. The movement caught the bull's eye and he spun. With a target now to vent his anger on, the bull pawed the ground, then lowered his head again and charged straight for Harley.

Stunned, Leighanna could only stare while Mary Claire's scream rent the air. "Harley! Watch out!"

But Harley didn't move. Already racing for the corral, Mary Claire screamed again. "Hank! Help him!"

Already aware of the situation, Hank was swinging the trailer's rear doors closed again. He jerked the latch in place, locking the other two bulls inside, then whirled and ran for the raging bull, yelling and flapping his hat.

Just before the bull reached Harley, he spun again, fixing his eyes on Hank. While the bull's attention was diverted, Mary Claire ducked between the corral gates and grabbed Harley's arms and started tugging and pulling him toward the side of the corral.

Leighanna ran to kneel on the opposite side and the two women pulled and pushed until they had dragged Harley beneath the corral's lowest rung and to safety. Breathing raggedly, and with sweat stinging her eyes, Leighanna glanced up just as the bull charged for Hank.

"Hank!" she screamed, scrambling to her feet. "Run!"

But Hank stood frozen in place, his face tense, his dark

gaze fixed on the bull. Just as the animal reached him, Hank lunged to the side, narrowly missing being gored by the bull's deadly horns by inches. The bull whirled again with a frustrated roar, his eyes wild, mucous swinging from his mouth.

Instinctively sensing Hank's intent, Mary Claire pointed to the gate behind him. "The gate, Leighanna! Open the gate!"

Seeing the gate on the far side of the corral, Leighanna ran for it. With her fingers trembling, she fumbled at the latch, managed to pull the iron pin free and swung the gate wide.

In the center of the corral, Hank stood, his back to her, waiting for the bull's next move.

Hoping to divert the animal's attention away from Hank as Hank had done for Harley, Leighanna boldly stepped into the opening and let out a yell, waving her hands over her head.

The bull lifted his head, and for a split second Leighanna looked straight into his eyes and knew what death must look like. She hollered again, and Hank twisted his head to look over his shoulder. She saw panic slip into the dark depths of his eyes when his gaze met hers.

"Get out of the way!" he yelled.

She started to turn away, but the bull chose that moment to attack. With a powerful lunge, he ducked his head and charged straight for Hank. Leighanna felt the ground beneath her feet reverberate with each pounding of his hooves against the hard-packed dirt, and the view before her slipped into slow motion. The bull slung his head, caught Hank in the stomach on the curve of his horn and sent him arcing in the air and over his back before he raced on for the opening. With a speed she hadn't known she possessed, Leighanna jumped out of the bull's way and swung the gate closed behind him as he raced past her, bucking, into the open pasture.

Quickly she slid the pin back into place and scrambled over the corral and ran for Hank, her heart in her throat. When she reached him, she dropped down to her knees on the ground beside him. "Hank! Are you all right?" she cried. When he didn't answer, she leaned over him and pressed a cheek against his chest, listening for a heartbeat. Murmuring a prayer of thanks when she heard one, she started to lift her head...and saw the ragged tear on his shirt. With shaking fingers she lifted the torn cloth and nearly fainted when she saw the blood oozing from the torn flesh.

"Oh, Hank," she cried, blinded by her own tears. "Please don't die."

"He's a lucky man," the doctor said with a shake of his head. "You both are."

Harley nodded, testing the bandage on his forehead with a tentative finger. "How bad's he hurt?"

"I've stitched up the hole in his side, but he's got a cracked rib that's going to take some time to heal. But my biggest concern right now is his concussion." The doctor blew out a frustrated breath. "I told him I wanted to keep him overnight for observation, but he pitched a walleyed fit. Says he's never spent a night in a hospital and doesn't intend to spend one now."

Harley chuckled. "Must not be hurtin' too bad, if he's complaining."

The doctor frowned at Harley. "He's hurting all right, he's just too damn stubborn to admit it." The doctor shook his head. "In the mood he's in, I'd be better off letting him go home. Is there anyone there to take care of him? He's going to have to be awakened on the hour for the next twenty-four and have an eye kept on him for at least another forty-eight.''

Harley stole a glance at Mary Claire, who stood beside him. ''No, but I guess I could take him home with me and care for him.''

Squaring her shoulders, Leighanna stepped forward. ''That won't be necessary. I'll take care of him.''

Both Harley and Mary Claire stared at her in surprise, but Leighanna firmed her lips and stubbornly met their gazes. ''It's my fault he was hurt. If he hadn't turned to look at me when I yelled, he'd never have been gored.''

''Now, Leighanna,'' Harley murmured soothingly. ''It's not your fault Hank got—''

Leighanna turned her back on Harley, ignoring him, and gave her full attention to the doctor. ''If you'd be kind enough to write out your instructions, I'll see that Hank follows them to the letter.''

Leighanna sat by the side of Hank's bed in a chair she'd dragged in from the bar, her back straight as a board, her gaze riveted on his face. Occasionally she'd tear her eyes away, but only long enough to check the clock she'd placed on the bedside table.

Four hours had passed since Harley, Mary Claire and the kids had left, leaving her solely responsible for Hank's care. Four long nerve-burning hours.

Thankfully, Harley had stripped Hank of his clothes and put him to bed before he'd gone, sparing Leighanna that difficult task. By the time she'd locked the doors behind them all, Hank's pain pills had kicked in and Hank was out like a light.

That first hour alone, Leighanna had used her time wisely, gathering all the supplies she thought she might need during the night. Water, ice stored in a small cooler, an alarm clock, a shallow bowl and a handful of wash-cloths, along with the medications and the instructions the doctor had written out for her.

For the next three hours she'd kept a vigil next to the bed, waking him each hour as she'd been instructed, al-ternately coaxing and bullying a response from him until she was sure he hadn't slipped into a coma as the doctor had warned he might.

Those minutes in between each wakening had been miserable for Leighanna as she stared at Hank's bruised face, reliving those nightmarish minutes in the corral, knowing that she was at least partially responsible for the injuries Hank had suffered.

He was so brave, so unselfish, stepping in front of that bull to save Harley's life. Few men would have done what Hank had done for Harley, she knew that. She re-membered the look in his eyes when he'd seen her stand-ing in the open gate, the fear, the panic. It was in that split second where he lost his concentration that he was left at the bull's mercy...and it was her fault, as surely as if she'd thrown him in the path of the raging bull. It was also in that split second, when the terror was clawing its way up her throat in a scream, that she'd known that what she felt for him wasn't platonic. Her feelings were seeded much more deeply than that.

Catching her lower lip between her teeth to stop the tears that spurted to her eyes, she leaned, catching a wisp of hair from his forehead. Tenderly she combed it back into place with her fingertips. "Oh, Hank, please be okay," she whispered. "I—" she caught herself before uttering the words of love that trembled on her lips.

Hank awakened, feeling as if someone were holding a branding iron to his side. Struggling against the darkness that sucked at him, he forced his eyes open a slit and saw a pair of dusty cowboy boots hitched on the foot of his bed. He opened his eyes a little wider and twisted his head slightly, just far enough to follow the line of crossed denim legs, to the man who sat slumped lazily in the chair beside his bed.

"What the hell are you doing here?" he grumped, fighting to bring Cody into focus.

Cody dropped his feet and lowered the chair to all four legs, grinning. "Nursing you."

Hank closed his eyes on a groan, remembering the accident with the bull and the trip to the hospital. He tensed when he remembered the gentle hands that had soothed him through the night. Opening one eye, he squinted at Cody suspiciously. "How long have you been here?"

"Oh, a couple of hours, I guess. Leighanna had to run over to Acres's office and sit through a briefing, discussing what all our fine mayor wants her to do for this shindig he's hell-bent on throwing. She said she wouldn't be gone long. She's planning on bringing all her stuff back here and working on it while she keeps an eye on you."

Hank eased out a breath of relief, thankful to know that it had been Leighanna's hands that had soothed him through the night and not Cody's.

Cody stood and poured water into a glass, then shook a pill from a bottle on the nightstand. "Leighanna said you were supposed to take this if you woke up." He held out the glass and the pill.

Hank shook his head, still feeling the effects of the last pain pill he'd taken. "Don't want any more of that stuff. It just makes me sleep."

Cody chuckled. "That's the idea." He gave Hank's hand a nudge. "Now bottoms up or Leighanna's gonna skin my ears for not following her instructions."

Hank frowned at his friend. "Tell you what. You help me get to the bathroom so I can take a leak, and I'll take the damn pill."

Cody puckered his lips, shaking his head slowly. "Leighanna specifically said that you aren't to get out of this bed. She left a jar right here," he said, leaning down to retrieve it, "for you to use when nature calls."

Hank narrowed an eye at Cody, letting him know what he could do with the jar. "Bathroom or no pill, which is it?"

Heaving a sigh, Cody offered an arm for support. "All right, but if you tell her I let you do this, I'll swear you're lying through your teeth."

Six

When Hank awakened again, he could tell by the slant of the sun against the apartment's only window that it was late afternoon. He could also tell that Leighanna had been busy.

A table from the bar had been moved into his apartment and situated in front of the west-facing window. A long phone line stretched from the kitchen counter where his phone was usually mounted to the table where it was now perched. Leighanna sat at the table with her back to him, speaking in a low voice to someone on the phone, obviously not wanting to disturb him.

Keeping still so as not to let her know he was awake, Hank watched her lift a weary hand to the back of her neck and rub.

"Yes, we can make arrangements to have electricity available in the field where you set up your carnival," he heard her say. She listened a moment, then said, "No problem. As long as you have everything set up by noon on the Friday before Labor Day weekend.'' Another pause, then, ''Thanks. I'll expect to hear from you then.''

With a sigh she replaced the receiver and fell back against the back of the chair, lifting her hair away from her neck, then pressing her hands upward in a spine-arching stretch. The curve of that back, the delicate stretch of those arms, did something to Hank's insides.

At that moment the alarm she'd positioned in the center of the table went off with an earsplitting ring. She dropped her arms and stretched across the table to hit the Off button. Twisting around in the chair, she turned a concerned eye to Hank...and found him watching her.

''It's okay,'' he murmured, his tongue still thickened by the drugs. ''I'm already awake.''

Leighanna was on her feet and scurrying to the side of the bed. ''Do you need anything? Are you in pain?''

Unable to keep his eyes open any longer, Hank let them close. ''No, I'm fine.'' He licked his dry lips. ''A drink of water might be nice, though.''

Leighanna picked up the pitcher she'd placed on the nightstand and quickly poured half a glass. Slipping a hand under his head, she lifted him and pressed the glass to his lips. He drank long and deep. ''Thank you,'' he murmured, sinking back against the pillows.

''While we're at it,'' Leighanna said, ''you might as well take your pills.''

Hank shook his head. ''Can't,'' he said, struggling to try to sit up. ''Got to get to the bar.''

Leighanna pressed a hand against his chest. ''Don't worry about the bar. We're taking care of everything.''

Too weak to argue, Hank sank back against the pillow. ''Who's 'we'?'' he asked, squinting to keep her in focus.

''Harley is tending the bar, Mary Claire is manning the

grill, and Stephie and Jimmy are going to help me serve and clear the tables.''

Hank closed his eyes, his lips curving in a wobbly smile. "Takes that many to replace me, huh?''

Leighanna chuckled. "Yes, that many.'' She took the bottles and shook out the required pills before replacing the tops again. "Here,'' she said, taking his hand in hers and pressing the pills against his palm.

Though his eyes remained closed, a soft smile tugged at one corner of his mouth. "What do I get for taking them?''

"A headache and an infection if you don't,'' she replied, dryly.

"But shouldn't I get some kind of reward for being a good patient?''

"Like what?'' she said, smiling at his boyishness in spite of her weariness.

He sighed. "A kiss would be nice.''

Chuckling, she gave his hand a nudge, relieved that he felt well enough to tease her. "Take the pill and we'll see.''

Dutifully, Hank lifted his head, popped the pills into his mouth and grinned crookedly at Leighanna over the rim of the glass before washing the pills down with water.

As soon as she removed the glass, he settled back against his pillows, closed his eyes and puckered up.

Without hesitation, Leighanna leaned over and pressed her mouth to his. All the fear, all the worry she'd carried for the past few hours drained from her as his lips moved on hers. He might be hurt and he might be half out of his mind with drugs, but he still had the power to weaken her knees with something as simple as a kiss. When at last she drew away, Hank sighed again.

He opened his eyes and looked at her. "You know what I hate most about these pills?" he asked.

"What?"

"They make me sleepy."

Leighanna laughed softly, leaning close to wipe a smear of lipstick from his lips. "That's what they're supposed to do."

"I know," he said on a sigh heavy with regret. "But at the moment, there's something I'd a lot rather do than sleep."

Leighanna turned off the lights in the bar and made her way back to the apartment in the darkness, yawning. She was exhausted. After two days without sleep and with putting in a full day of work at two jobs, she was bone dead tired.

She quietly opened the door to the apartment, then tiptoed to the side of the bed. The lamp was on, and in its glow she could see that Hank slept peacefully. Sitting down on the chair beside the bed, she eased her tennis shoes off her feet and bit back a moan of relief. After checking the clock, she noted that she had another thirty minutes before it was time to wake Hank and give him his medication.

I'll just close my eyes for a minute, she told herself, and rested her forehead against her hands on the bed next to Hank.

When the alarm went off thirty minutes later, it was Hank who hit the Off button. Leighanna never moved so much as a muscle. The sight of her keeping vigil—even if she was sleeping—made Hank's heart go soft. He'd never had anyone watch over him, even as a child. The idea that Leighanna would, touched him like nothing in his life ever had before.

Pressing his hand to his stitches to keep from tearing his wound open, he shifted, turning on his side so that he could see her better. Carefully, he smoothed her hair away from her face. The toll of caring for him while holding down two jobs was evident in the dark circles beneath her eyes, in the depth of her sleep. She'd spent two nights at the side of his bed caring for him, or so he'd been told. Personally, he didn't remember much about the past forty-eight hours, though he did remember the touch of gentle hands and a soft, feminine voice that pulled him from his sleep, then soothed him back into it again.

Knowing how uncomfortable she must be, sleeping like that slumped against the side of the bed, Hank shook out his pills and quickly gulped them down with water, then turned and gave Leighanna a gentle nudge.

"Leighanna," he whispered, lowering his face close to her ear.

"Hmm?"

"Come on, sweetheart," he urged gently, slipping her hand from beneath her head and giving it a gentle tug. "Come on up here." He scooted over, making room for her on the bed, while keeping up the gentle pressure on her hand.

More asleep than awake, she let him guide her onto the bed, then immediately curled up into a ball at his side, fitting her hands beneath her cheek.

Unable to resist, Hank moved closer, laying his head next to hers, and rested his arm in the gentle curve of her waist.

Sighing, he closed his eyes and slept.

Leighanna awakened slowly to the feel of warm, moist breath blowing rhythmically against her cheek and the weight of an arm draped loosely at her waist. She opened her eyes to find Hank watching her.

"Good morning," she said sleepily.

"It is that," he replied, a slow grin curving at his mouth. "Did you sleep well?"

"Yes, I—" Suddenly her eyes flipped wide as she gained full consciousness. Panicked, she tried to sit up, but Hank kept her in place with the weight of his arm.

"Your medicine," she cried, managing to twist around far enough to glance at the clock. "I didn't hear the alarm! You've got to—"

"Relax," he soothed. "I've already taken it."

"You did?" she asked, twisting back around to look at him.

"Yep, I did."

Relieved to know that she hadn't truly failed in her duties, that Hank had followed the doctor's instructions, she dropped her head on the pillow and let out a long sigh of relief.

And realized where she was.

Her eyes rounded as she peered at Hank, suddenly aware that she wasn't on the chair, but in the bed with Hank. "What am I doing up here?" she asked in a shocked whisper as she inched away from him.

Chuckling, he tightened his arm around her. "Don't worry," he soothed. "You only slept." He drew her next to him again, then winced slightly at the strain the movement placed on his cracked ribs.

"Oh, Hank," she said, popping up. "Did you hurt yourself?"

"Just a little," he said, and placed a hand on her cheek, forcing her head to the pillow next to his. "Want to kiss it and make it better?"

Relieved that he hadn't done any damage to his

wounds, Leighanna laughed at the teasing in his voice. "You can't be hurting that much if you've got kissing on your mind."

His eyes warmed, taking on that seductive hue. "Oh, I'm hurting alright. And you know what hurts the most?"

Unable to resist touching him, she smoothed a stray lock of hair from his forehead. "What?"

"The fact that I've finally got you where I want you and I'm too banged up to do a damn thing about it."

Hank's apartment had taken on the look of a war zone. Sticky notes were stuck to every available surface, a huge map of Temptation's downtown area was tacked to the wall with different colored pins, representing God knew what, poked at strategic points across its surface. In the center of it all, Leighanna sat at the table she'd set up—a pencil stuck in the roll of hair she'd piled on her head, and the phone receiver pressed to her ear—while she flipped through the organized chaos in front of her.

From his spot on the bed, Hank had a bird's-eye view of all the goings-on, even if it was a little blurred by the medication he'd been taking. He had to give Leighanna credit, he thought with a shake of his head. The woman was an organizational whirlwind. In just three days, she'd taken all of Mayor Acres's grandiose plans for the festival and made them a reality, at least on paper. Committees had been set up, a carnival arranged and a variety of activities planned to take place throughout the downtown area during the two-day event.

"Yes," she said into the receiver, "I have that information right here." She quickly selected a card from those fanned on the corner of the desk and read the information to the party on the other end of the line.

He watched as she replaced the phone. "How can you

make sense of all this stuff?'' he asked with an expansive wave of his hand.

Leighanna turned to him, smiling. ''Because I know exactly where everything is.'' She stood and walked to the side of the bed, reaching, as was her habit, to smooth a hand across his forehead, then drawing it tenderly down the side of his face. Touching him had become so natural over the past few days that she didn't give a thought to the intimacy it suggested. ''How are you feeling?''

''Like a caged lion,'' he grumped. ''I want out of this bed.''

Leighanna tipped her head in sympathy. ''I know you're miserable, but by tomorrow you should be strong enough to be up and around for a little while.'' She glanced toward the dresser, the only other substantial piece of furniture in the room. ''Would you like me to turn on the television?''

Hank snorted in disgust. ''There's nothing on but soaps and those damn ridiculous talk shows.''

Chuckling, Leighanna took his hand in hers and squeezed. ''Well, what can I do to help you pass the time?''

Hank glanced at her, arching a brow. ''I could think of a thing or two.''

After spending three days with him, Leighanna had grown accustomed to his constant teasing and only laughed. ''I swear, you have a one-track mind.''

''Yeah,'' he said, pulling her down beside him. ''But at least I'm consistent.''

Sighing, Leighanna settled in the crook of his arm, stretching her legs out beside his. ''You are that.''

He placed a finger beneath her chin and angled her face to his. His gaze moved over her face as he slowly traced the line of her jaw. "Has anyone ever told you how beautiful you are?"

Leighanna's cheeks burned in embarrassment, but she was secretly pleased by his compliment. "You're only saying that because I'm the only woman you've seen in the past three days."

"No. It's the truth." He twisted slightly until he faced her. "But the hell of it is, you're beautiful inside and out. I've never met a woman like you before."

"Hank, that's awfully sweet, but—"

"Shh," he said, pressing a finger at her lips. "Don't argue, just say thanks."

Smiling, she pulled his finger away. "Thanks."

He tucked his hands beneath his head and settled next to her, smiling, too. "Wanna mess around?"

Leighanna chuckled. "You wish."

He sighed, closing his eyes. "Yeah, I do."

Thinking he was going back to sleep, she started to rise, but he pressed an arm at her waist, stopping her. She twisted around to look at him, but his eyes remained closed. "Don't go just yet," he murmured.

"But you need to rest."

He tightened his arm around her, pulling her back down beside him. "So do you."

She did nap, but not nearly as long as Hank. When she awakened, he was still curled at her side, his arm slung around her waist, their heads resting on the same pillow. Unable to resist touching him, she smoothed a lock of hair from his forehead and gently finger combed it back into place. He's getting to you, she warned herself. His vulnerability due to his injuries, his constant teasing when they both knew he didn't have the strength to follow through, his care for her own welfare when he'd insisted that she rest with him the night before and again today.

One more day, she remembered with more than a little regret. One more day and Hank would be up and around and strong enough to care for himself. One more day and she'd be spending her nights at Mary Claire's again. The thought saddened her.

Easing from beneath his arm, she allowed herself one last look at his handsome face, at the muscled strength of his bare chest exposed above the sheet that covered him. Sighing, she turned away and headed back to her makeshift desk and the work that awaited her.

In the darkness Hank lay on what he'd come to think of as his prison—his bed—and listened to Leighanna's movements coming from the other side of the bathroom door. The sound of the shower running, the whisk of clothes as she peeled them over her head. The muffled click of the shower door as she closed it behind her. Her soft sigh of contentment as she stepped beneath the water. He could imagine her there with the water sluicing over her upturned face and streaming down between her small, taut breasts. He could almost smell the soap as she lathered it over her body.

The thoughts were so vivid, the images they drew so clear, he felt his groin tighten with desire. He wanted her, had wanted her from the first day he'd laid eyes on her. But that wanting had taken on an urgency over the last few days. Sighing, he folded his hands beneath his head. Tonight, he told himself. He'd thought about it all day and, stitches and cracked ribs or not, tonight he would make her his.

The water shut off and Hank tensed, listening as he monitored her movements. When the bathroom door at last opened, he quickly laced his hands over his chest and closed his eyes, feigning sleep. He heard her soft footsteps, smelled that utterly feminine fragrance that was so much a part of her as she drew near the bed. Then he felt the silkiness of her touch as she gently laid a hand against his forehead. He'd grown used to her touch, missed it when she wasn't near.

Moving slowly so as not to startle her, he took her hand in his and drew it to his lips. He heard her soft gasp when his lips met the sensitive center of her palm, and he smiled.

Her soft laugh wafted to him through the darkness. "I thought you were asleep," she teased gently.

"I was." He drew her to sit beside him on the bed and wished he had more than moonlight, so that he could fully see her face. "But I woke up when I heard you in the bathroom."

"And I was trying so hard to be quiet. I'm sorry."

"I'm not."

Nerves danced to life beneath her skin at the huskiness in his voice. "You're not?"

"No."

A sigh shuddered out of her as he gently guided her to lie down beside him.

"What's all this?" he asked, angling so that he could catch the folds of her silk nightgown between his fingers.

"I got tired of sleeping in my clothes. I had Mary Claire bring me a few things so that I could change."

"Ummm." He brought the fabric to his cheek and rubbed. "Soft," he murmured appreciatively. He laid a hand against the thigh he'd exposed beneath the silk fabric. "But not as soft as you."

Leighanna's breath snagged in her chest. His fingers skimmed her thigh, gradually moving higher, and she was sure she would suffocate beneath the sensations that spiraled through her and knotted her lungs. His other hand moved to mold her face.

"Leighanna," he murmured, his breath blowing warm at her lips. "I want to make love to you."

His statement didn't shock Leighanna, nor did it frighten her, for she wanted the same thing. Had wanted it for days now. "But Hank, your stitches, your ribs," she reminded him gently.

His touch on her heated flesh never once wavered. "I think I can manage if we're creative."

Trembling now, Leighanna tried to imagine what he meant by creative. But then his lips met hers, and her mind went blank, and she gave herself up to the heat that flamed to life between them. His hand slipped higher, dragging her nightgown up her legs, then higher still, until it was twisted at her waist. His hand drifted to the mound of her femininity and with a moan of pleasure, he cupped her, molding her with his strong hand.

His fingers stroked, lighting fires between her legs that caught and flamed upward, spreading throughout her abdomen. She arched against him, hungry for more than just his touch.

"Leighanna, beautiful Leighanna," he murmured, drawing back to look at her face in the soft moonlight. "I want to please you. Tell me how."

"I...I don't know," she whispered desperately, then gasped when his finger slipped between the velvet folds and found the center of her core.

"Then I'll show you."

Releasing his hold on her, he caught her nightgown in his hands, pulled it over her head and tossed it to the floor. Before she could draw the first ragged breath, his fingers found her again in the darkness and he lowered his face to her breasts. Taking a nipple between his teeth, he suckled, slowly drawing her in, while the stubble of his beard rasped against her bare flesh. His tongue teased, his fingers probed and Leighanna was sure that she would die of frustration unless she could touch him, as well.

Reaching out, she found his chest and moaned softly in sympathy when her fingers grazed the strip of gauze that covered his wound and the wide strips of tape that bound his ribs. Careful not to hurt him, she eased past it, sliding her hand in a downward journey, enjoying the feel of the coarse hair that veed below his navel and gasping when her hands bumped against his arousal. Timidly she touched him. He shifted, giving her better access and moaned his pleasure against her breasts when her fingers instinctively wrapped around his hardness.

"Don't be shy, Leighanna," he murmured against her heated skin. "Do whatever feels natural."

Boldly she let her hand slide down until her knuckles grazed the coarse hair nesting at the base of his staff. The movement incited her as much as it did Hank, and she repeated the motion again and again, until they were both breathless.

"Leighanna," he groaned, shifting again until his body was flush against hers. "You're killing me."

Emboldened by his words, she sought his mouth, mimicking with her tongue the movements of her hands on him until he tore his mouth from hers, gasping. He'd planned this all day, lying in his bed, dreaming of a slow seduction. But now with her there, lying naked next to him on his bed, with her clever hands playing over his swollen staff, he knew he'd never last. "I want you now," he said fiercely. "Now!"

Leighanna knew a moment of uncertainty. Not that she didn't want him, too, but she wasn't at all sure how they could proceed without hurting him. She lifted her gaze, seeking his in the moonlight. "But how?"

In answer, he caught her by the waist and turned her, fitting her buttocks tight against his groin, spoon fashion. With his lips at her ear, murmuring to her, he guided her until his manhood pressed at the moist folds of her femininity. Gathering her in his arms and holding her tight against him, he pressed a hand at her abdomen and eased inside.

She gasped at the first feel of him and arched against him, unconsciously drawing him further inside. "That's right, baby," he murmured against her ear. "That's the way." Then he began to move against her, slowly at first, but gradually increasing the speed and the rhythm, guiding her with his body until she raced along with him.

The heat increased, blinding Leighanna to everything but the feel of him inside her. Colors pressed against her closed lids, flashing sharper and sharper, gathering into a tight ball until they exploded into shattering white. Crying out his name, she arched hard against him, thrusting her hips in the curve of his groin…then bonelessly melted against him, absorbing the shudders of release that tore through him, as well.

His hand came around to cup her breasts and his nose nuzzled at the smooth column of her neck. Never in her life had Leighanna felt so utterly weak, yet so sated.

"Oh, Hank," she whispered, covering his hand with her own. "I never knew it would be like this."

His breath moved her hair in a sigh. "Neither did I," he murmured. Gathering her even closer, he said again, "Neither did I."

Thursday afternoon Leighanna glanced up from her work at the grill to see Hank leaning against the door frame, watching her. For the first time since his accident, he was standing upright and fully dressed.

Catching up a dishcloth, she quickly dried her hands, smiling as she crossed to him. "Just look at you," she teased, carrying a hand to his cheek. "You've even shaved."

A grin chipped at one corner of Hank's mouth as he covered her hand with his own. "For you," he murmured. "I was afraid if I rubbed you raw with my stubble, you wouldn't let me near you."

She laughed softly, smoothing her hand down his cleanly shaven jaw. "Oh, I don't know. There's something to be said for a man with a beard."

"Then I'll grow it back," he promised, lowering his face toward hers.

Leighanna stretched to her tiptoes to accommodate him, wondering how, with the night they'd spent, she could thirst for him so. But the touch of his lips on hers reminded her of just exactly how. Wrapping her arms around his neck, she gave herself up to the heat that pulled at her.

The front door banged open. "Hey, you two! Cut that out. There are innocent children approaching."

With her arms still looped around Hank's neck, Leighanna tore her mouth from Hank's and turned to see Harley, standing just inside the entrance to the bar and wearing a broad smile. Her cheeks burning in embarrassment, she quickly dropped her arms and tugged her shirt back in place just as Mary Claire and her children stepped around Harley.

At the shocked look on Mary Claire's face, Leighanna struggled to think of an explanation. "We were just—"

"Kissing," Hank finished for her, and slipped an arm around her shoulders, not in the least embarrassed to be caught in what he considered such a natural act. "Don't tell me these kids have never seen anyone kiss before."

Stephie looked up at Harley, her future stepfather, and beamed a smile. "'Course we have. Harley kisses Mama all the time."

"Gross," Jimmy muttered, and headed for the juke-box.

Hank tossed back his head and laughed. "The day'll come," he warned, "when you'll be wanting to kiss a girl."

Jimmy made a gagging sound and slipped a quarter into the jukebox. "I'd rather kiss a pig," he muttered, studying the selections.

"You'd have to catch it first," Stephie sassed as she skipped across the room to join her brother. Before Jimmy could stop her, she punched in a number.

The slow, seductive thrum of guitars wafted across the room before Clay Walker added his voice to the music, singing, "Hypnotize the Moon."

Jimmy rolled his eyes. "Jeez, Stephie. Why'd you pick that sappy song? You know that's Mama's and Harley's favorite?" Without waiting for a reply, he stuffed his hands in his pockets and trudged off with Stephie trailing close behind. The back door slammed once, then quickly opened and slammed again as Stephie kept up a fast pursuit.

A man accustomed to taking advantage of an opportunity when it presented itself, Harley caught Mary Claire's hand in his. "How about a dance?"

Smiling lovingly up at him, she stepped into his waiting arms. She closed her eyes as she rested her head in the crook of his neck, losing herself in the music and the lyrics as he slowly danced her around the room.

On a wistful sigh, Leighanna folded her arms at her

breasts and watched them. Seeing the dreaminess in her expression, Hank shifted, turning her into his arms. "Do you dance?" he asked softly.

Immediately, she tensed and lifted her gaze to his. "Yes, but I've never danced to Country music. I—"

Before she could refuse him, Hank guided her arm around his waist and caught her other hand up in his. "It's not that much different," he instructed gently. "Just follow my lead."

And she did, just as she'd done the night before when he'd led her in an entirely different dance. She let him draw her close until the length of her body pressed close against his, the pressure of his thigh squeezed between her legs. Laying her head against his chest, she felt the familiar thud of his heart against her cheek and knew that she'd follow him anywhere. He danced her around the perimeter of the long, narrow room, adroitly dodging tables and occasionally Harley and Mary Claire's blended forms while Clay Walker seduced them all with the words of his song.

Hank tipped her face to his without missing a step. "You're like her, you know," he said, his voice husky as he gazed down at her.

"Who?" Leighanna murmured, lost in the depths of those dark brown eyes that looked so deeply into her own.

"The lady in the song. You, too, can charm the stars and hypnotize the moon just by walking into a room."

And Leighanna lost a little more of her heart to him.

Seven

The bar had been unusually crowded for a Thursday night, a result of a rodeo being held in nearby Bandera. Though only a few customers remained, Leighanna worried about Hank holding up to the unaccustomed pace after lying flat on his back for the past three days.

Mary Claire had already gone home, taking the children with her, but, thankfully, Harley had insisted on staying until closing time, obviously not wanting Hank to overdo things on his first day back at work. For that Leighanna would always be grateful, because she knew that without Harley there, Hank would have insisted on carrying his share of the workload and probably ended up suffering a relapse.

As she glanced Hank's way again, she noticed that his face seemed a little more pale that it had before. Picking up the tray of dirty glasses she'd just gathered, she headed his way, determined to make him go to his apartment and rest.

Setting the tray on the corner of the bar, she moved to stand beside him. Without a thought to the customers still in the bar who might be watching, she lifted a hand to his cheek and angled his face to hers. Her heart nearly broke at the sight of the fine lines of weariness that fanned from the corners of his eyes.

"Hank, darling," she murmured in concern. "You've done enough for one night. You need to be in bed."

His smile softened as he hitched a hip against the counter and turned to her, closing his hand over hers. "Only if you're there with me."

Leighanna huffed out a breath, then laughed, shaking her head. "If I thought you'd truly rest, I would."

"Hank Braden!" a woman's voice called. "Is it true what I've heard, that you've taken up bullfighting?"

Leighanna thought she felt Hank's fingers tense over hers, but then his hand was gone and he was turning away.

"Well, hello, Betty Jo," he said, and planted his hands on the bar. "What are you doing in our part of the world?"

Betty Jo? Leighanna's heart stopped, then kicked against her ribs as she recalled why the name sounded familiar. The barrel racer from Marble Falls, whom the men in the bar had teased Hank about when Leighanna had first started working at The End of the Road.

Swallowing hard, she turned to look at the woman standing just inside the entrance to the bar. A mane of wild, red hair corkscrewed from beneath a wide-rimmed black hat, and a breast-enhancing vest showed a generous view of cleavage, while she stood with her hands fisted on hips cemented beneath skin-tight jeans. Her eyes fixed on Hank, a huge smile on her face, Betty Jo headed for the bar.

"Rode barrels over at Bandera tonight," she said, her hips rocking suggestively with every step she took. "Thought I'd stop in here before I headed my trailer for home and see if you might need some cheering up after the run-in you had with the bull."

When she came to a stop opposite Hank, she leaned across the bar, offering an even more alarming view of her breasts. With a sultry smile, she took his cheeks between her hands, drew his face slowly to hers and covered his mouth with her full lips.

Sucking in a shocked breath, Leighanna took a step back, then another, and bumped into Harley who stood at the grill, watching, too. Whirling, she braced her hands on his arms to keep from stumbling and lifted her horrified gaze to his. In his eyes she saw not the shock that she felt, but only pity. Her cheeks flamed in embarrassment as she remembered that only hours before, Harley had caught Hank kissing her. Whirling again, she ran for the kitchen.

Once there, she pressed her palms to her hot face, willing away the tears that threatened. She wouldn't cry, she told herself fiercely. She'd known what Hank was like. She'd heard the rumors about his reputation, had even experienced his captivating charm firsthand. He was a rounder, a man who thought nothing of drifting from one woman to another without a thought to the one he left behind. Unfortunately, during the days alone with him in his apartment, she'd forgotten that well-known fact and allowed herself to fall prey to his seductive tactics.

But not any longer, she vowed.

Forcing herself into action, she stabbed the stopper into the sink and turned on the water, squeezing a liberal dose of dishwashing liquid beneath its spray. Grabbing a tray-ful of dirty glasses, she propped it on the edge of the sink and started sinking glasses beneath the growing mountain of bubbles.

By the time she'd washed her way through three trays of dirty dishes, she'd calmed somewhat and felt more in control of her emotions. At least she knew she wouldn't cry.

"Leighanna?"

She heard Hank's voice behind her, but refused to turn around. "Yes?"

"Are you okay?"

She rammed the dishrag into a beer mug and swirled furiously, but forced a tone of indifference in her reply. "Why shouldn't I be?"

Hank noted the tenseness in her shoulders, the angry jabbing of her arms into the dishwater. He knew she was angry, and knew what had brought on the mood, but didn't have a clue what to do or say to make things better between them. Damn Betty Jo, he cursed silently. Why'd she have to show up tonight of all nights?

"Leighanna, Betty Jo is—"

"A very striking woman, isn't she?" Leighanna finished for him.

Hank stepped up behind her and laid a hand on her shoulder. "Not as pretty as you," he murmured, dipping his lips to her neck.

Leighanna lifted her shoulder to shrug off the mean-ingless caress. "And what a figure!" she continued as if he hadn't spoken, then stretched to place the mug on the drain board. "Did you get a load of those breasts? I re-member you saying you preferred a woman with large breasts. I'd say she's just about the perfect size for you."

"Leighanna..."

She dragged the stopper from the sink and snatched up the towel to dry her hands. Hoping to escape him before she humiliated herself further by allowing him to see her cry, she brushed past him. "If you'll excuse me," she said. "I need to mop the floor."

Hank caught her before she'd taken a full step. Whirling her around, he clamped his hands on her shoulders, and, using his thumbs beneath her chin, forced her face to his.

He saw the glimmer of tears and knew he'd hurt her. "Leighanna, I'm sorry."

"Sorry?" she repeated, forcing a laugh. "Whatever for?" Ducking beneath his arms, she grabbed for the mop bucket.

Angry now himself, Hank snatched it from her hands. "For God's sake, Leighanna, the floor can wait until tomorrow."

"Fine," she said, and headed for his apartment door. "I'll just get my things and get out of your way."

Hank stared at her back, panic tightening his chest. With a frustrated growl, he tossed aside the bucket and stomped after her into the apartment. "Where do you think you're going?"

She snatched her nightgown from the bedpost where she'd tossed it earlier that morning and stuffed it into a bag, trying her best to avoid his gaze. "Mary Claire's. There's no reason for me to spend the night any longer. You're more than capable of taking care of yourself."

"But, Leighanna, I want you to stay."

Angry that he would think she was that easy, that free with her affection, she whirled, her eyes blazing. "Three's a crowd, Hank."

"If you're talking about Betty Jo," he said hesitantly, "she's gone."

Leighanna tore her gaze from his and marched to the bathroom, raking her toiletries from the countertop and into the bag. ''Well, I'm sure that if you feel the need for more *company,* there are other women that you can call.''

Hank grabbed her as she brushed past him again and spun her around, sinking his fingers into her shoulders. He gave her a hard shake. ''What is wrong with you? There isn't anyone else that I want to call. I want you!''

Leighanna pressed her hands over her ears, unwilling to listen to his lies. The tears that had threatened broke through, streaming down her cheeks.

At the sight of them, Hank hauled her into his arms, but before he could offer any comfort, Leighanna was bracing her hands against his chest and shoving for all she was worth.

''No!'' she cried, backing away from him as she dragged her hands to her eyes. Before she could disgrace herself any more, she snatched up her bag and all but ran for the door.

Leighanna sat at the kitchen table with her hands pressed against her face, wishing with all her heart that she'd never been born.

''I hate him,'' she mumbled against her fingers. ''I hate him, I hate him, I hate him.''

''You don't mean that,'' Mary Claire scolded. ''You're just upset right now.''

Leighanna tore her hands from her face and slammed them into fists against the top of the table, making Mary Claire jump. ''You're darn right I'm upset,'' she cried as she pushed herself from the chair to pace Mary Claire's kitchen. ''You should have seen her. She had on these jeans that were so tight I'm sure she had to lie down on the bed just to get them zipped. And her boobs," she raged on, holding out her hands a good foot in front of her chest. "They stuck out to here and you *know* how much Hank likes boobs!"

Mary Claire bit back a smile. "No, I'm afraid I don't."

Leighanna whirled on her. "Well, he does. Trust me." She paced away again, tossing her hands in the air. "And then she kisses him! Right there in front of God and everybody, she lays this lip-locker on him that had his eyes bulging out of his head and smoke coming out his ears!"

Mary Claire had already heard this story, or at least she'd heard Harley's version of the story, and was having difficulty making the tales mesh. "And this made you angry?"

Leighanna spun to look at Mary Claire, her eyes sparking in righteous indignation. "Well, of course it made me angry! Wouldn't it you?"

"That would depend on how I felt about the man being kissed."

Leighanna felt heat crawl up her neck, and she quickly turned, pacing away again.

"You're in love with him, aren't you?"

Leighanna stumbled to a stop, her spine arching as if she'd just suffered a blow there. Slowly, her shoulders slumped in defeat. "Yes," she murmured pitifully. "And I hate him."

Mary Claire nodded sagely, her heart going out to her friend. "The two emotions can sometimes be confused."

Leighanna crossed back to the table and dropped onto the chair opposite Mary Claire, fresh tears budding in her eyes. "What am I going to do?" she moaned.

"What do you want to do?"

Leighanna wearily wagged her head. "I don't know,"

she said, sniffling. "He wanted me to stay with him, but I couldn't, not after what he did."

"And what exactly did he do?"

Leighanna lifted her head, looking at Mary Claire in amazement. "Well, he kissed her, that's what!"

"Did he kiss her, or did she kiss him?"

Leighanna frowned, not liking the direction of Mary Claire's gentle probing. "Well, he certainly didn't put up much of a fight," she muttered defensively.

"And neither did you," Mary Claire replied, looking at Leighanna from beneath an arched brow. Her expression softened at the stricken look on Leighanna's face. Taking her friend's hand in hers, Mary Claire sought to soothe. "It would be foolish to think that Hank didn't have a life before he met you. And even more foolish to let his past stand between you and what you so obviously want."

The silence was painful, pricking at the back of Leighanna's neck and making her nerves burn in frustration. She'd tried to fill it over the past few days by smiling and chatting with the customers that drifted in and out of The End of the Road, but the silence was still there, stretching between herself and Hank like a wire strung too tightly.

Even when away from Hank and working at Mayor Acres's office she felt the oppressive silence. She'd transferred all her things from Hank's apartment back to the mayor's office, but every time she looked at them, she was reminded of him and his apartment and the hours they'd spent together while she'd simultaneously nursed him and planned the festival. Though it had been a strain on her physically, she'd enjoyed caring for him, laughing with him, loving him, and would give anything to be able to return to those days when everything was so easy between them, so relaxed.

Wearily she rubbed a hand across the back of her neck. She hadn't slept a total of four hours since the night Betty Jo had appeared at the bar. And with the exhausting schedule she was maintaining, working for both Hank and the mayor, the lack of sleep was taking its toll.

Sighing, she stripped off her apron and retrieved her purse from beneath the bar. She stole a glance at Hank where he stood before the cash register, calmly counting the night's proceeds. Emotion wedged in her throat at the mere sight of him, nearly choking her.

Had Mary Claire been right, she wondered, when she'd suggested that Leighanna should have put up a fight for Hank?

No, she told herself and gave herself a hard shake. She'd done the right thing in leaving. She refused to be just another notch on his bedpost.

"I'm leaving," she said, hoping that he'd at least look her way.

But Hank never so much as lifted his head. He merely grunted his acknowledgment and went on with his counting.

Though he remained behind the bar, his gaze fixed on the money spread before him, Hank followed the sound of Leighanna's departure: the squeak of her tennis shoes on the freshly mopped floor, the click of the door handle as she twisted it open and the soft shoosh of wind that swept inside before she stepped through and closed the door behind her again.

"Damn!" he muttered, tossing the money aside. "Damn, damn, double damn, hell!"

He raked his fingers through his hair, turning away

from the sight of her retreating figure. He couldn't stand much more of this silence. The woman was slowly driving him nuts! She sashayed around the bar, laughing and talking with his customers, but she treated him as if he wasn't even there. When she did bother to address him, it was with a coolness that bordered on disdain. He had retaliated with the same, refusing to knuckle under to what he considered her female coercive tactics.

And what in the hell had he done to deserve her silent snubbing, anyway? Nothing! he told himself. Absolutely nothing! Was it his fault that Betty Jo had decided to pay him a visit? Hell, no! And was it his fault that Betty Jo had plastered herself all over him? Absolutely not! He'd been an innocent victim, trapped between a woman with whom he'd enjoyed a short, if memorable, fling and the woman who currently had his heart caught in a wringer.

He paused, listening, waiting for the sound of that clunker of Leighanna's to spark to life, but heard nothing but silence. Silence again, he thought with a growl of irritation. And he was damn sick and tired of the silence. Striding to the door, he peered through the glass. In the corner of the parking lot, Leighanna stood at the front of her car, spotlighted by the security light, struggling to lift its hood.

"What in the—" He jerked open the door and marched across the parking lot, grinding gravel beneath his boots with each angry step.

"What in the hell do you think you're doing?"

Leighanna lifted her head, wearily pushing her blond hair from her face as she turned to look at him. He'd finally spoken to her, but, naturally, it was only to curse her. "It won't start," she said miserably, then bent her head over the open hood again.

Hank huffed an impatient breath, then moved closer to

look over her shoulder. He shook his head at the grimy condition of the engine and the tangle of baling wire that seemed to hold everything in place. "No wonder," he muttered in disgust. "When was the last time you had this hunk of junk worked on?"

When Roger fleeced me of my money when he took it to have the transmission repaired, Leighanna remembered morosely. But she wouldn't tell Hank that. She was sure he already considered her a fool, after the way she'd reacted to Betty Jo, and she wasn't about to prove him right. "About a month before I moved here," she said instead.

Hank grunted, shouldering her out of his way. "Give it another try," he ordered gruffly as he bent his head over the engine.

Reluctantly Leighanna slipped behind the wheel and turned the key. *Waaaa...waaa...waaa.* "Come on," she urged, pumping the accelerator, "please start."

But in spite of all her prodding and Hank's tinkering under the hood, the engine refused to turn over. Biting back tears of frustration, she climbed from the car.

Hank watched her out of the corner of his eye, seeing the weary slump of her shoulders, the dark circles beneath her eyes, the glimmer of unshed tears...and his anger melted away. "Why don't you go to my apartment and put your feet up? As soon as I get it started, I'll give you a holler."

Too exhausted to argue, Leighanna turned and headed back to the bar.

Hank watched her and swore under his breath. "She's going to kill herself if she keeps up this pace," he muttered as he ducked under the hood again. "If I don't wring her pretty neck first."

Hank had known it would be a waste of his time, but he tried his damnedest to get Leighanna's car running for her again. After fooling with the cantankerous engine for over an hour, he finally admitted defeat, slammed down the hood and headed for the bar.

After locking the door behind him, he stopped in the kitchen long enough to wash the grease from his hands, then walked on to the apartment, ready to offer Leighanna a ride back to Mary Claire's.

But when he opened the door and found her curled on his bed asleep, he didn't have the heart to wake her. Knowing full well that she'd probably be madder than a wet hen when she awakened and found herself in his bed, he left her there and went into the bathroom, closing the door softly behind him. He stripped off his clothes, then stepped inside the shower and twisted on the faucet, letting the cold beads of water sting his face. With a shiver he adjusted the temperature to a warmer setting, then moved it right back, deciding a cold shower might be what he needed after all.

When he finally climbed into bed beside her, Leighanna rolled, curling against his chest in her sleep. With a sigh Hank hooked an arm at her waist and pulled her close.

"Leighanna? Sweetheart, wake up. It's time to go to work."

Leighanna fought the intrusion to her sleep and dragged her pillow over her head. "Go away," she mumbled.

Hank chuckled and lifted the edge of the pillow just high enough to see her face. "Can't. Not until you're on your feet and alert."

Leighanna swatted at his hand, but refused to open her eyes. "Leave me alone," she grumbled.

Hunkering down beside the bed, Hank raised the pillow higher and waved a steaming cup of coffee beneath her nose. She lifted her head, though her eyes remained closed, and sniffed.

"Is that coffee I smell?"

Chuckling, Hank kept the cup just out of reach. "Open your eyes and see for yourself."

Though it was an effort, Leighanna forced her lids open, squinting against the sunshine streaming into the room. Moaning, she reached for the cup and grasped it between her palms. "Thank you," she murmured before taking the first greedy sip. Hiking herself up to a sitting position, she eased back against the headboard, gradually taking in her surroundings. "I take it I fell asleep," she said with a self-conscious glance at her wrinkled clothes.

Hank dropped down on the foot of the bed. "Passed out would be more like it."

She lifted her gaze to his, remembering her reason for being in his apartment. "My car?"

He snorted. "What car?" Then waved away her look of concern. "Don't worry, I've already called Mitch. He's on his way over to tow it to his garage."

Her eyes widened in alarm as she lurched to a sitting position. "But I've got to go to work at the mayor's office!"

Hank deftly snagged the coffee cup before she succeeded in spilling the hot liquid all over herself. "Don't worry. I'll take you."

Hank sat parked at the curb in front of the mayor's office with a picnic basket resting on the seat beside him.

Nervously he drummed his fingers against the steering wheel while he waited for Leighanna to appear.

He'd never taken a woman on a picnic before, which in itself was a little daunting. The fact that Leighanna knew nothing of his plans and might very well refuse to go with him only added to his nervous state.

But Hank was determined to make things right between them. When he'd driven her to work earlier that morning, the atmosphere had been a little strained. *A little strained,* he reflected, choking back a laugh. That was an understatement. She hadn't said more than two words to him during the drive to Mary Claire's, where she'd quickly showered and changed clothes and mumbled only a quick "thank you" before she'd leapt from his truck and hauled ass into Acres's office like the devil himself was chasing her. And that bugged Hank enough to want to do something about it.

The whole picnic setup screamed of courting, and truth be known, Hank had never courted a woman in his life, had never felt the need to do so. In the past women had flocked to him, and he'd never had to put forth much effort to pursue one. Not that he was pursuing this one now, he told himself. He just wanted to set things right between them again.

At least he would if she ever showed her face beyond Acres's door. He glanced at the clock on the dash. The woman had to eat sometime, he told himself in growing frustration. He'd give her another five minutes and if she didn't appear, he'd—

At that moment the door to the mayor's office opened and Leighanna stepped through, shoving a pair of sunglasses across the bridge of her nose. She stopped cold when she saw Hank's truck parked at the curb.

He stretched across the seat and rolled down the window. "Need a ride?" he asked.

"W-w-well, no," Leighanna stammered, wondering why he was there. "I was just going to walk over to the mercantile and grab something for lunch."

Hank pushed open the door. "No need. I've got enough here for two." He pulled the basket to his side, giving Leighanna room. When she hesitated, he dipped his head down to peer at her. "You like fried chicken, don't you?"

"Well, of course I do," she sputtered. "Everybody likes fried chicken."

"Then what are you waiting for." He patted the seat beside him. "Climb in."

Not at all sure what was going on, Leighanna climbed onto the seat and closed the door, eyeing the picnic basket suspiciously. "You cooked fried chicken?"

Hank shifted into drive and eased away from the curb. "No. Mary Claire did."

Leighanna rolled her eyes heavenward. She should have known that her friend was behind this. "So this was Mary Claire's idea," she said wryly.

Hank glanced at her, pressing a hand over his heart as if wounded. "No, it was mine. I was over at Mary Claire's with Harley, helping him fix that leaky pipe in the upstairs bath, and Mary Claire was in the kitchen frying chicken. You know how she is," he added, turning his attention back to the road. "She cooks for a damn army. She invited me to stay for lunch, but I told her, no, that I was coming over here to see if you needed a ride to lunch, and she insisted on making up this picnic basket."

Leighanna simply stared at him, unable to believe he

would do something so thoughtful. "How sweet," she murmured.

Hank gave his head a quick nod. "Yep, that Mary Claire's sweet, alright."

Leighanna rolled her eyes again, shaking her head. "No, silly. I meant you."

He twisted his head around to look at her and grinned when he saw her amused smile. "No, just selfish. I'm trying real hard to get back on your good side."

The door of resistance that Leighanna had slammed between them squeaked open a bit. Wanting to take advantage of the opening he'd offered, but unable to meet his gaze, Leighanna dipped her chin. "Hank, I'm sorry. I know I overreacted when I saw…well, when I saw Betty Jo—"

Before she could finish, he stretched across the seat and caught her hand, squeezing it within his own. "You don't have anything to be sorry about. You reacted just fine." He chuckled, taking the wheel with two hands again as he turned his attention back to the road. "In fact, if the situation had been reversed, and I'd been forced to watch some strange man kissing you, I might have been tempted to rearrange the guy's face."

Leighanna bit back a smile. "The thought did cross my mind."

Hank tossed back his head and laughed. "Lucky for Betty Jo that you didn't." He cocked his head to look at her and shot her a wink. "As I recall, you've got a mean right hook."

Leighanna saw the gleam of humor in his eyes and let that door of resistance swing all the way open. "Yeah, I do, don't I?" she said smugly.

Leighanna neatly packed away the remains of their picnic, then turned and glanced at Hank, who was stretched out on the blanket beside her, his hands folded beneath his head. The desire to lie down beside him was strong, but even though he'd made the first step in repairing the rift between them, Leighanna was hesitant to seek such an intimacy.

As if sensing her uncertainty, Hank withdrew a hand from beneath his head and held it out to her, palm up in invitation. With a sigh, Leighanna placed her hand in his and let him draw her to his side. Nestling her head in the crook of his shoulder, she snuggled against him, placing a hand on his chest. Beneath her fingers, his heart beat in a steady, comforting rhythm.

She'd missed this, she thought as the heat from his body permeated hers. Missed lying beside him, missed his constant teasing, missed the comforting warmth of just being near him.

"Leighanna?"

"Hmmm," she murmured, her voice lazy with contentment.

"I've been thinking.... You know, with your car out of commission and with you working two jobs and with that long drive out to Mary Claire's and all... Well, I was thinking that it might be easier if you stayed with me for a while."

Leighanna's fingers stiffened on his chest. Slowly she lifted her head high enough to look at him. "Stay with you?" she repeated, her heart thudding against her ribs, wondering what he was offering.

Hank raised his head, meeting her gaze. "Yeah. That way I could drive you to work and save you the hassle of having to find a ride back and forth every day."

Leighanna hadn't thought anything could hurt as much as seeing Hank kiss another woman. But she was wrong.

She scrambled to her feet, whirling away from him, then just as quickly back. "Just like that?" she cried, snapping her fingers. "You expect me to move in with you?"

Frowning, Hank pushed himself to an elbow, wondering what he'd said that had set her off. "Well, yeah," he mumbled uneasily. "Makes sense to me."

Leighanna fisted her hands at her sides, the implication behind his offer crystal clear in at least *her* mind. "You scratch my back, I'll scratch yours. Is that what you're thinking?"

Hank's frown deepened. "What in the hell are you talking about? I just asked you to move in with me. I don't recall saying anything about scratching anybody's back."

"Well, that's what you intend, isn't it? You taxi me around, and in exchange I'll serve your more basic needs?"

The hurt in her voice slowly registered. Without meaning to, once again Hank had screwed up royally. He pushed himself to a sitting position and dragged his hands down his face. With a sigh, he looked up at her. "No, Leighanna, that's not what I had in mind at all." Determined not to let this misunderstanding stretch into another war of strained silence, he reached out and snagged her ankle, hauling her down across his lap. Before she had a chance to react, he locked his arms tight around her, holding her in place, though she stubbornly refused to look at him.

He pressed a finger beneath her chin, forcing her gaze to his. "I've never asked a woman to move in with me before. And you're sure as hell not making this first time very easy." He heaved a frustrated sigh when she continued to glare at him. "The deal about your car was just an excuse. I want you to move into my apartment, for no other reason than I want you with me. It's as simple as that.''

Though she tried to hang on to her anger, Leighanna felt it slipping away, giving way to another emotion, one that responded to the sincerity in the brown eyes that gazed down into hers. "But, Hank. It isn't simple. It's—"

"What I want," he finished for her. "And what I think you want, too." He shifted, settling her more snugly in his lap. "I've never asked a woman to live with me before, never felt the need to until now." He laid a hand at her cheek and drew his fingers downward in a slow caress. "But I'm asking you, Leighanna. Only you. Tell me that's what you want, too."

Eight

Digging his fingers through his hair, Hank paced his small apartment, silently cursing himself under his breath. He should have gone with her, he told himself. He should've never allowed her to go to Mary Claire's without him to pack her things. What if during the drive she had second thoughts and decided she didn't want to move in with him after all? What if Mary Claire convinced her that moving in with him was a mistake?

A sound outside had him spinning toward the window. Leaning to peer through the glass, he saw Leighanna climb down from his truck. Heaving a sigh of relief, he charged for the side door located in the bar's kitchen.

"Here, let me," he said, taking the suitcase from Leighanna's hand. He felt the tremble in her fingers and was glad to know he wasn't the only one suffering a bad case of nerves. He glanced over her shoulder, then back at her. "Is that all?"

She smiled shyly, and the innocence in that smile touched a spot on Hank's soul he hadn't known existed. "Yes," she said softly. "Most everything I own is in storage in Houston."

He held the door, allowing her to pass in front of him. "I guess we won't be fighting over closet space, then, huh?" he teased, hoping to put them both at ease.

He set the suitcase on the floor, and Leighanna immediately reached for it. He stilled her with a touch of his hand. "That can wait," he said, his voice growing husky. He wove his fingers through hers. "First, I thought I'd give you a tour of your new home."

Leighanna glanced up at him in surprise, then laughed as she scanned the small room. "I don't think that's really necessary, do you?"

"Oh, very," he said in mock seriousness. Dragging her behind him, he crossed to the kitchen nook. "This is the kitchen," he said, then gestured to a closed door. "And that is the bathroom." He took three steps, tugging her along behind him. "And this," he said with an expansive wave of his hand, "is the bedroom."

Laughing fully now, Leighanna turned to him, grateful to him for recognizing the awkwardness she was experiencing and allaying it with his teasing. "Nice place you have here, Mr. Braden."

His lips curved in a slow grin as he wrapped his arms at her waist and pulled her to him. "I like to think so." He lowered his head to hers. Their lips touched, then touched again, and Leighanna sighed, stretching to loop her arms around his neck as that familiar warmth spread through her abdomen.

His hands dipped to cup her bottom, drawing her fully against his groin, and the swell of his manhood settled in the curve of her pelvis…and Leighanna truly felt as if she'd at last come home.

"You know, I'd really like to make love with you right now," Hank murmured, brushing the tip of her nose with his. "But I sure wouldn't want you to think that's the only reason I invited you to move in here."

Leighanna chuckled, sliding her hands from around his neck. "Since I want that, too, I could hardly accuse you of taking advantage of me."

With a provocative smile, she slid her hands from his neck, found the first button on his shirt and won a moan from him as she quickly worked it through its hole. Smiling against his lips, she slowly moved her hands down his chest, freeing each button until his chest was fully bared. Loving the feel of him beneath her inquisitive fingers, she pushed his shirt over his shoulders and smoothed her hands across the muscular expanse she'd bared, her fingers lightly grazing the tape that still wrapped his ribs. At his waist, she tugged open the snap of his jeans, then slowly unzipped them, thrilling at Hank's sharp intake of breath when her knuckles grazed the swell of his manhood.

"I want to make love with you," she whispered against his lips as she took him into her hand.

"I think that was my line," he replied, his breathing ragged.

Leighanna chuckled and increased the pressure of her fingers around him.

"Oh, Leighanna," he moaned as she stroked him. "You're killing me."

She gave his chest a shove, pushing him down on the bed. "Prepare to die, then, because I'm not planning on stopping anytime soon." Hiking her skirt up in her hands, she followed him down, straddling him while she sought his mouth again.

And Hank was sure that somehow, when he wasn't looking, another woman had snuck into his room and into his bed. This couldn't be Leighanna. Not his Leighanna. The Leighanna he knew was shy and totally unaware of her feminine power. Whereas, *this* woman was aggressive, a seductress bent on having her way with him.

And Hank couldn't have been any more willing to give her what she wanted.

Hooking his thumbs in the waist of her skirt, he dragged it over her hips and down her legs, taking her panties along with it, then just as quickly divested her of her blouse and tossed it all carelessly to the floor. On a moan of sheer pleasure, he felt her hips meet his, the mound of her femininity grinding against that part of him that throbbed for her. Impatient for the feel of her honeyed softness around him, Hank grasped her hips within the span of his hands and lifted her, guiding her to him. She gasped at the first urgent thrust and dropped her chin, her long blond hair falling to curtain her face, then tossed it back, passion building on her face and in the blue eyes that gazed down at him.

Flattening her hands against his chest, she rode him, taking her pleasure from him and giving a ton of it in return. Hank felt the pressure building and cursed his own lack of control. He wanted this to last forever, this feeling of oneness, this building of passion that blinded him to everything but the woman he held in his arms. But the sight of her before him, her cheeks flushed with the passion they shared, her skin beneath his roving hands slick with perspiration, her swollen breasts swinging only inches from his face, was more than he could withstand. Reaching out, he grasped her breasts in his hands and drew her to him, catching a nipple with his teeth and drawing her deep into his mouth. She arched, crying out, and he felt the pulsating heat of her climax tighten around him, drawing him with her to that razor-sharp edge.

With a shudder that wracked his body from temples to toes, he slipped over that edge, spilling into her. With a groan, he released her breast, but only to seek her mouth with his. Folding his arms around her, he drew her to his chest. Her breath warmed his neck on a sigh of utter contentment...and Hank wondered why he'd let his stubbornness allow so many days to pass without mending the rift between them. He'd missed her, and not just for the sex. He'd missed *her*, her gentleness, her softness, the strength of her spirit. Tightening his arms around her, he pressed his lips to her hair, not wanting to let her go.

"Hank!" Leighanna called. "Breakfast is ready!"

Fresh from a shower, Hank tugged on his jeans and opened the bathroom door. Leighanna stood before the stove, wearing one of his shirts, and from what he could tell, nothing beneath it. Crossing to stand behind her, he nuzzled the back of her neck with his nose. "Ummmm. Smells good."

Smiling, Leighanna levered a heaping stack of pancakes onto a plate and turned to hand it to him. "Me or the pancakes?" she teased.

Hank took the plate, grinning. "Both." He dipped his face over hers to steal a quick kiss, then turned and headed for the bed.

"And where do you think you're going with that?"

Hank stopped and turned to find Leighanna standing where he'd left her, her arms folded beneath her breasts, her mouth curved in a disapproving frown. "To bed to eat," he said innocently.

She lifted a hand and pointed. "That's what tables were made for."

Hank followed the direction of her finger and discovered that Leighanna had been busy while he'd been in the shower. She'd dragged a table in from the bar again, and shoved it underneath the window. A vase of sunflowers sat in the center of the table and two places were set on opposite sides.

With a guilty smile, he detoured by the bed and crossed to the table. "Sorry. Old habit."

She nodded her approval as he placed his plate on the table, then fixed her own and moved to sit opposite him, neatly sidestepping her still-unpacked suitcase. Picking up the bottle of syrup, she squirted a generous amount over her pancakes...then shivered when something cold brushed her bare toes. Snapping up her head, she looked at Hank and saw him grinning at her. "What are you doing?" she asked as that 'something' smoothed a slow path up her leg, sending ripples of heat skimming all the way to her abdomen.

"Touching you." He popped a forkful of pancakes in his mouth, still grinning. "I'm not used to having a beautiful woman around in the morning. Just checking to make sure it wasn't a mirage."

Laughing, she reached beneath the table and gave his foot a playful shove. "Trust me, I'm no mirage."

His grinned softened, taking on a seductive look. "No," he said, and slipped his foot between her knees to tease her thighs apart. "I can definitely tell you're real. I can feel your pulse beating."

Already feeling herself weakening, Leighanna struggled to breathe. "Your breakfast," she reminded him, with a gesture toward his plate, then gasped when his toe gently prodded the juncture of her thighs.

His eyes turned a smoky brown and he laid his fork aside. "I'm not really very hungry, are you?"

Leighanna had only been in the apartment a week, but she was slowly making her presence known. Dresses, skirts and blouses added about a foot and a half of color to Hank's otherwise dreary closet. With Hank's permission, she'd claimed the top right dresser drawer as her own, relegating his underwear and socks to a lower drawer. Three pots of geraniums bloomed on the window sill above the table, and the refrigerator, once holding only the bare necessities—a gallon of milk and a six-pack of beer—was now filled with fresh vegetables, fruits and a covered dish containing a leftover meat loaf.

Hank shook his head as he turned his gaze to the bed. He couldn't remember the last time his bed had been made up. Probably never, he thought with a chuckle.

The only thing in the room that remained the same was the television propped up on the dresser for easy viewing from the bed. But he figured she'd change that, too, if she ever figured out how to fit a sofa into the small apartment.

But he didn't mind the changes, he told himself as he stripped off his shirt. In fact, he kind of liked the homey look his apartment had taken on since Leighanna had moved in. Eating regularly wasn't so bad, either, he reflected as he gave his flat stomach a sound pat. And, boy, could that Leighanna cook. He figured he'd put on a good five pounds in the week that she'd been there.

As he pulled a fresh shirt from the closet in preparation for the arrival of his poker buddies, he heard the shower shut off and smiled. The nights weren't too bad, either, he thought with a flicker of anticipation. Going to sleep with Leighanna curled at his side and waking up with her in the morning...well, a man could get used to that.

At that moment the bathroom door opened and Leighanna stepped out, her skin flushed from the heat of the shower...and Hank's mouth went slack. Dressed in a blue satin nightgown that matched her eyes and dipped into the provocative shape of a heart between her breasts, she crossed to him, the satin gown whispering against her bare skin. His mouth suddenly dry, he cupped his hands at her shoulders and drew her to him, burying his nose in the silky tresses of her hair.

"Wow," he murmured appreciatively. "What's the occasion?"

She lifted a hand, cradling his cheek and stepped back to look up at him, her eyes filled with a warmth that made Hank's blood heat. "We're celebrating. Tonight is the anniversary of our first week together."

Hank tensed, remembering his poker game. He hadn't thought to mention it to Leighanna, wasn't in the habit of sharing his plans with anybody but himself. He lifted his wrist behind her head and glanced at his watch. If he hurried, he might be able to call the boys and tell them the game was off for the night.

"Leighanna, sweetheart," he began. But before he could finish the statement, he heard the clump of boots outside his apartment door. A loud knocking followed.

"Hank? You in there?" Cody called.

"Hurry up!" Harley echoed. "I'm feeling lucky tonight!"

Leighanna's expression turned from dreamy to dismay in the time it took to bat an eyelash. "What are they doing here?" she whispered.

Hank lifted his shoulder in a self-conscious shrug. "It's our poker night." When he saw her face fall in disappointment, he hurried to reassure her. "But don't worry, I'll get rid of 'em."

He started to spin away to do just that, but Leighanna caught his arm. "No. Don't. We can celebrate another time."

"But, Leighanna..."

She tipped her face to his, forcing a smile to hide her disappointment. "No, really. I don't mind." She gave him a gentle shove toward the door. "Now go on and strip those men of all their money."

Blue, red and white chips lay clumped in the center of the table, sharing the space with several empty long-neck beers. Four men sat around the table, their backs slumped, while a fan of cards blocked their faces.

Cody smiled beneath the cover of his cards, then plucked several chips from the pile in front of him. "I'll see your ten, and raise you five."

Harley glanced up from his cards to frown at Cody. "If you've got another damn straight, I'm gonna have to shoot you for the cheater you are."

Cody chuckled. "Don't have to cheat to beat you."

Frowning, Harley tossed the required chips down on the table. "I call."

Fanning his cards out on the table, Cody revealed three kings, the four of spades and the ace of hearts. He let out a whoop of victory and grabbed for the pile of chips.

Harley snagged his wrist. "Not so damn fast." He nodded to the other two men. "What've you got, Newt?"

The tall, rangy cowboy just wagged his head and tossed his cards on the table. "A lousy pair of threes."

Harley turned his attention to Hank. "How 'bout you, Hank? What've you got?"

When Hank didn't respond, but kept staring at the door

to his apartment, Harley gave him a sound kick under the table. "You in this game or not?"

Hank shook his head to clear the vision of Leighanna dressed in nothing but shimmering blue satin, lying on his bed, waiting. "Yeah, I'm in," he said, forcing himself to focus on the cards in his hands. He reached for a chip. "I'll raise you five."

Harley shook his head sadly. "Man, you've got it bad. Can't even keep your mind on a poker game."

Hank frowned, noticing for the first time the cards spread face up on the table. "Just tired, is all." He stood, kicking back his chair. "In fact," he said, faking a yawn and stretching his hands above his head, "I think I'm going to call it a night. You guys stay as long as you want, just lock up before you leave."

He turned away and strode for the outside door, the three men staring at him in puzzlement.

"You suppose he's so lovesick that he's forgotten the way to his own apartment?" Cody asked.

At that moment, the door opened again and Hank strode back in with a fistful of sunflowers clutched in his hand. With three sets of eyes boring into his back, he ducked behind the bar, nabbed a bottle of wine from the rack there, then headed for his apartment.

Harley tossed down his cards. "Well, I'll be damned," he muttered. "Never thought I'd see the day that old Hank would let a woman get between him and a poker game."

Hank stepped into the apartment and closed the door softly behind him. The only light in the room came from the television screen where an old movie played, but in its glow he could see Leighanna nestled against his pillow, her back to him, her shoulder rising and falling in the even rhythm of sleep.

Flicking off the television, he set the bottle of wine and the bouquet of sunflowers on the nightstand and quickly stripped out of his clothes. Grabbing the bouquet and tucking it behind his back, he buried a knee in the mattress and leaned over her. "Leighanna?" he called softly.

"Hmmm?" she murmured sleepily.

"Wake up, sweetheart," he urged gently.

She rolled to face him, pushing herself up on an elbow and opening her eyes to a squint. "What is it?" she asked, trying to bring him into focus.

"I have something for you." He drew the bouquet from behind his back and held them out to her. "Happy anniversary, sweetheart."

Leighanna's throat tightened at the sight. "Oh, Hank," she murmured tearfully, reaching for them. "How sweet."

He leaned to brush his lips across hers. "No, just crazy about you."

"Oh, Hank..." She dropped the flowers and threw her hands around his neck.

He gathered her close, sliding down her length until he lay beside her. He leaned back and combed his fingers through her hair, looking at her upturned face in the moonlight. He'd only been away from her a couple of hours, and that was only as far as the other room, yet it felt like years since he'd seen her, touched her. "I missed you," he said, his voice husky.

She smiled softly, catching his hand in hers and drawing it to her cheek. "I missed you, too."

He let his hand slip from beneath hers, following its descent with his gaze until his fingertips rested against her satin-covered breast. He slipped his hand inside the point of the heart, cupping her. "You're so soft," he murmured as if to himself. "So fragile." He flicked a nail over her nipple and watched it swell. Unable to resist the puckered tip, he dipped his head, taking her nipple between his teeth. "And so sweet," he whispered as he drew her deeper into his mouth.

Leighanna settled against the pillow on a sigh, offering herself more fully to him. Catching a wisp of hair from his forehead, she combed it back, enjoying watching the muscles in his jaw move as he suckled. Tears brimmed in her eyes. She loved him. The admission didn't frighten her as it once might have. She trusted Hank. Even with something as precious as her heart.

His suckling strengthened and she thrilled at the sensations he drew. They seemed to spiral in a red-hot line from her breast to burn at her deepest feminine core. No one had ever loved her so thoroughly, she thought, as her breathing grew ragged. No one had ever taken her so far so fast.

His fingers skimmed the satin fabric covering her abdomen and trailed down her leg until he found the gown's end. He lifted his head from her breast and looked at her, and she nearly wept at the longing she saw in his eyes. "As pretty as this piece of nothing is," he said, a slow smile curving at one side of his mouth. "I prefer your skin." Catching the hem, he drew it up, waiting while she lifted her arms for him, then raised himself to a kneeling position so he could peel it over her head.

Moonlight spilled over her body, and Hank sank back on his heels on a sigh. Reaching out, he touched a finger to her lips, then her breast, then let it drift slowly over the gentle swell and down to the mound of femininity at the juncture of her thighs. "So beautiful, Leighanna. So, so beautiful,'' he murmured before pressing his lips just below her navel.

Delicious shivers chased down Leighanna's spine as he pressed his hot lips against her fevered skin. Moaning her pleasure, she dug her fingers into his hair, needing that contact, no matter how slight. He wet his fingertip in her growing moistness, then gently separated the velvet folds of her femininity. Finding the button of her desire, he pressed and she gasped, bucking beneath his hand.

''Hank!'' she cried almost desperately, then groaned again, arching, her back bowed as she sought an even more intimate touch.

Pressing hot kisses across her abdomen, he returned to her, crushing his mouth against hers, stabbing his tongue between her parted lips, mimicking the rhythm of his hand on her.

Desire clawed its way through her and, nearly crazed with her need for him, for release from the demons he'd unleashed inside her, Leighanna dragged her nails down his back, urging him to her.

With a feral growl, he slipped between her legs, kneeling, his manhood throbbing with the desire to make her his. Taking her hips in his hand, he lifted, gently guiding her until she was impaled on his staff...but even that wasn't close enough. He reached for her, bringing her body to his chest, crushing her against him as he began to move inside her. Perspiration beaded on their skin, blending as their bodies chafed with each wild thrust.

''Hank!'' she cried, clawing at his back as the tension built to an almost unbearable crescendo. ''Oh, Hank...''

''It's okay, baby,'' he soothed, clinging to that last thread of control. ''Let it go. I've got you.''

Because she trusted him, she did let go. She gave herself up to the void that sucked at her, knowing that he was with her every step of the way. His lips found hers in the darkness and she clung to him, nearly weeping with joy as shudders wracked his body, as his seed spilled hotly into her and her own climax exploded around him.

Tucking an arm behind her waist, he guided her down, then quickly reversed their positions so that she lay on top of him. Tucking her head beneath his chin, he pressed his lips to her hair.

Her heart filled to near bursting with her love for him, Leighanna lifted her head to look at him. Moonlight kissed his features, adding beauty to an already handsome face. "I love you, Hank," she whispered. She felt his body tense against hers and his fingers still on her hair.

"I care for you, too, Leighanna," he murmured.

His inability to say the words she longed to hear in return didn't hurt as she might have expected, because it was there, in his eyes, suppressed beneath his guarded expression. His love for her. She knew that a man like Hank who had never experienced love would have difficulty voicing his feelings. But he'd said he cared for her, and she knew he did. For now, at least, that would be enough. In time he would learn to trust her love for him and would find the courage to share his feelings with her, as well.

Sighing, she laid her head against his chest, content to wait for that moment.

Hank stood with his shoulder pressed against the open bathroom door, his hands tucked beneath his armpits, sporting a pout as big as the state of Texas. "How long are you going to keep this up?" he mumbled dejectedly. "You're hardly ever here."

Leighanna's hand froze on the mascara wand and she

shifted her gaze from her own reflection in the mirror to Hank's...and had to smile. "Just a few more days," she promised, and quickly popped the wand back into the tube and laid it aside. With a last fluff of her hair, she turned to him. "By Saturday night the festival will be over, and my life will get back to normal."

He flattened himself against the door as she brushed past, then trailed her into the tiny apartment. "What's normal? This is all I've ever seen. You flitting in and out, then collapsing into bed, too exhausted to do anything but sleep."

Shrugging into a linen jacket, Leighanna turned, unable to suppress the laughter that bubbled up at the miserable expression on his face. "Oh, you're deprived, all right," she said dryly.

Hank had the grace to blush, knowing full well that they made love every night and sometimes managed to squeeze in a nooner or an afternooner before the bar opened. And that was without considering those early morning trysts. "Well, so I exaggerated a bit," he admitted grudgingly. "But that doesn't mean I wouldn't like to see a little more of you."

Laughing, Leighanna caught his cheeks between her hands. "I don't know how you could possibly see any more of me," she said, arching a knowing brow. Giving him a quick kiss, she whirled away. "Gotta run, or I'm going to be late."

And with that she was gone, leaving Hank with nothing but the lingering scent of her perfume to haunt him and time on his hands.

"Hank!" Leighanna exclaimed as she burst through the front door of the bar. "Hank! Where are you?"

Hank strode from the kitchen carrying three cases of beer. "Right here. Where's the fire?"

"Oh, Hank! You aren't going to believe this," she gushed, her eyes bright with excitement as she climbed up onto a stool.

Hank levered the cases of beer onto the bar opposite her, then pulled out his knife to split the top box open. "Believe what?"

"Mary Claire and Harley are going to remodel Harley's house and they're going to move there after they marry!"

Hank looked at her, frowning, wondering what was exciting about that bit of news. "So?"

"So-o-o," she repeated dramatically. "Mary Claire is going to lease out her house again!"

Hank knew a moment's uneasiness, fearing where this conversation was headed. Pulling a beer from the box, he buried it in the ice, wishing he could bury his head there, too, and avoid this discussion.

"We could lease it from her," she continued, totally unaware of Hank's growing state of discomfort. "Just think," she sighed as she collapsed against the back of her stool, her eyes going dreamy. "A home. A real home, with room for both of our things. I've always dreamed of living in a house with a little white picket fence wrapped around it, with a place to plant flowers and maybe a small garden. Oh, Hank," she cried, sitting up straight and clasping her hands over her heart. "Isn't this wonderful?"

Hank slowly reached for another beer, averting his gaze from her expectant one. It didn't sound so wonderful to him. *Picket fences. Flowers. A garden.* The next rattle out of the box would be marriage. The whole setup reeked of commitment, and Hank was a little weak in the commitment department. It had taken all his nerve just to ask her to move in with him.

"What's wrong with where we live now?" he asked, frowning.

"W-well, nothing," Leighanna stammered, surprised by his lack of enthusiasm for her plan. "It's just that your apartment is so...well, so small. If we were to move into Mary Claire's house, then I could get my things out of storage. I don't have near enough furniture to fill that big house, but we could—" She broke off when she saw the storm clouds building on his face. "Is something wrong?" she asked, her stomach tying itself into knots.

"I'm not moving."

"But, Hank—"

"If you want to move," he ground out as he yanked a beer from the box, "fine, then move. But I'm satisfied right where I am."

His words were like a knife tearing through her heart. "Do you want me to move?" she whispered.

Hank slammed the beer onto the counter. "Hell, no, I don't want you to move. I'm satisfied with things just as they are. *You're* the one who's talking about moving."

Though still confused by his anger, Leighanna felt the knots in her stomach slowly unwind. He didn't want her to move, he was just scared, just as he was afraid to tell her he loved her. Slowly she stood, bracing her feet on the stool's rung. "It was just an idea. That's all." She leaned across the bar and wrapped her arms around Hank's neck. "It doesn't matter where we live. Wherever you are," she said, hugging him to her, "that's where I want to be, too."

Nine

Sounds from the festival drifted through the open door of the temporary office where Leighanna worked, distracting her from the long column of numbers she was double-checking. Giving up for the moment, she dropped her pencil and lifted her hair from her neck, sighing as the night breeze wafting through the open door cooled her damp skin.

Rearing back in the chair, she hooked a sandaled foot on the edge of the desk and stared through the window in front of her. Though darkness shrouded the area surrounding it, the park that lay beyond the small trailer was lit up like the sky on the fourth of July. Neon lights in a multitude of colors blinked on and off, luring fun seekers to lose their money on one of the games of chance, or their stomachs on one of the carnival's heart-stopping rides. Though it was nearing eleven and closing time, an amazing number of people still strolled through the carnival, eating cotton candy or holding a stuffed animal they'd won at one of the game booths.

I did it, she thought proudly as she watched the scene from the privacy of her office. Mayor Acres's festival is a success. And hopefully, she thought as she dragged her foot from the desk and picked up her pencil again, her life would get back to normal and she could spend more time with Hank.

"Leighanna?"

She stiffened at the sound of the husky and familiar male voice that came from behind her. Sure that she was mistaken about the identity of the person, she slowly turned, looking over her shoulder. But there he stood, his hands braced against the doorjamb, his hip cocked in that stance she knew so well. She squeezed her eyes shut, willing the image away as she would a bad dream, but as she did, his scent drifted to her. Polo. That spicy, sexy cologne he always wore. She forced her eyes open to find him watching her. A shiver chased down her spine.

"What are you doing here, Roger?"

He smiled that slow seductive smile of his and lifted a shoulder as he stepped inside the trailer. "I came to see you."

Leighanna spun back around, yanking up her pencil as she bent her head back over her work. "Well, you've seen me. Now leave."

"Leighanna, baby," he murmured as he crossed to her. "You don't mean that."

"Yes, I do, Roger. Now leave, or I'll call the sheriff and have him toss you out."

His hands lighted on her shoulders, and Leighanna stiffened as his fingers started a slow massage. He lowered his face to nuzzle her neck. "Come on, baby," he purred, making goose bumps of revulsion pop up on her skin. "You know you don't want to do that."

Leighanna bolted from the chair, whirling to glare at him. She lifted a hand, pointing a threatening finger at him. "You stay away from me, Roger. I mean it."

He lifted his hands, palms up in surrender. "All right. Whatever you say."

But instead of leaving as she'd hoped, he dropped down in the chair she'd just vacated, calmly studying the contents on the top of her desk. Leighanna lunged for the stack of money she'd just counted and quickly stuffed it into a zippered bank bag.

He slowly spun the chair around and Leighanna backed up a step, hugging the bag to her chest. Roger simply watched her as he propped his elbows on the chair's arms and templed his fingers beneath his nose. "Looks like you've done all right for yourself," he said with a nod toward the bag. "You've hit on a two-bit town just ripe for a picking."

Leighanna tightened her grip on the bag, knowing full well what he was thinking. "It isn't mine. I just work here."

He nodded sagely. "Yes, but who would be the wiser if you slipped a few of those bills into your purse?"

Leighanna's chin came up at his implication. "*I* would know."

He chuckled, then, and dropped his hands to lace them across his chest as he reared back in the chair. "Same old Leighanna. Honest as the day is long."

"And I see you haven't changed, either," she replied, her tone scathing. "You're still looking for easy money."

"Now, Leighanna," he chastened gently as he stood. "You know you love me."

She took a step back, recognizing that familiar gleam in his eye. "You're wrong, Roger. I don't love you. I'm not sure that I ever did."

"Oh, baby," he crooned softly as he lifted a hand to

her cheek. "We were good together. It could be that way again. All we need is a little nest egg to buy us that house you always wanted."

Once she might have melted at his touch, at his promises, but now she felt only disgust. As she looked at him, she wondered how she could ever have thought herself in love with this man, and worse, how she could ever have compared Hank to him. Hank was nothing like Roger, he was good and kind and giving, nothing at all like the schemer she was confronted with now.

Slapping his hand away, she ground out, "In your dreams, maybe."

Roger arched a brow, obviously surprised by this new strength in his ex-wife.

"Leighanna?"

Leighanna whirled at the sound of the voice behind her. "Hank!" she cried, guilt flooding her cheeks with heat.

He took a step inside the trailer, his gaze going from Leighanna to the stranger who stood behind her, then back to Leighanna. "Is there a problem?"

She forced a bright smile and quickly shook her head. "No. No problem." She twisted her head around to frown at Roger. "In fact, he was just leaving."

Though Roger's expression never once wavered, Leighanna knew him well enough to read the anger behind it. He gave her a tight nod. "It was good seeing you again," he said as he strode for the door. "Maybe we'll have a chance to get together again before I leave town."

Hank stepped out of the way to let the man pass. He watched him until he disappeared into the darkness outside the office, then turned his gaze back to Leighanna's. "Would you mind telling me what that was all about?"

Leighanna quickly shook her head. "It was nothing." Hoping to divert his attention from Roger, she hurried to the safe and placed the money bag inside. "It's almost eleven, isn't it?"

"Yeah," Hank murmured, frowning at her back. "The carnies are shutting everything down."

She straightened, raking her hair from her face with trembling fingers as she turned to look at Hank. "I'll be a while, yet. I still have some work to do."

Hank didn't have a clue what was going on, but he could see Leighanna's nervousness and wondered at it. "You're sure you're okay?" he asked again.

"Positive." She looped her arm through his and walked him to the door. "Are you going home now?"

"Yeah. Soon as I help Cody make a sweep through the park to make sure everyone's gone home."

She stretched to her tiptoes and pressed a quick kiss to his frowning lips, then changed her mind and deepened it. Hank was taken aback for a second at the urgency, at the almost desperation he tasted in her, but willingly gave himself up to her needs.

When at last she withdrew, she did so with a sigh that bordered on regret. "Don't wait up," she said, brushing a finger across his lips. "I'll probably be late."

She watched Hank as he walked away from the trailer, his hands shoved deep into his jeans pockets, then turned her gaze on the darkness beyond. A shiver chased down her spine. She knew Roger was out there somewhere. Waiting. Watching. She shuddered, drawing her hands up to rub at the goose bumps on her arms.

Why is he here? she wondered, choking back tears. Was he broke again and looking for money? She knew he'd seen the cash before she'd stuffed it into the bag. For Roger, that would be temptation enough to hang around.

Gulping, she turned and quickly closed the door, locking it behind her.

* * *

Hank did wait up, or at least he tried to, wanting and needing answers to the questions Leighanna had avoided before, but he finally fell into an exhausted sleep. When he woke up, the television was still on. Cartoons were now playing instead of the John Wayne movie he'd been watching when he fell asleep, and bright sunshine streamed through the apartment window.

With a frantic glance at the empty bed beside him, he rocketed from the bed and ran for the window, looking for Leighanna's car. His heart thudded to a stop when he discovered that it wasn't parked in its usual spot next to his truck.

"What in the—" Fearing that that damn unreliable car of hers had quit on her again and that she was stranded somewhere, he bolted for the bed. He snatched his jeans from the bedpost and yanked them on, then grabbed his shirt and shrugged it on. But when he stopped at the kitchen table to grab his keys, he saw it. A note propped against the vase of fading sunflowers he'd brought to Leighanna on their anniversary.

His fingers shaking uncontrollably, he picked it up.

"Dear Hank," he read. "I made a mistake in coming to Temptation. I'm going back to Houston. Please know that I will always love you." His eyes quickly scanned the note again, his heart slowly sinking. At the bottom it was signed simply, "Leighanna."

She'd left him. Without a word of explanation other than this sorry note...but then he remembered the man he'd seen her with in the trailer the night before.

It was good seeing you again, he remembered him saying. *Maybe we'll have a chance to get together again before I leave town.*

Anger surged through him, searing the wound on his heart. Curling the paper in his palm, he wadded it into a tight ball, then threw it as hard as he could against the opposite wall. It ricocheted back, rolling to a stop at his bare feet.

"Damn you, Leighanna," he roared, kicking at the wad of paper and sending it flying again. "Damn you for doing this to me!"

Sagging against the table, he squeezed his forehead between the width of one hand, fighting back the tears that burned in his throat, choked by the same emotions he'd suffered as a child each time his mother had left him behind.

They gathered at The End of the Road, just as they had so many times in the past to discuss this newest tragedy to befall Temptation. Mayor Acres stood at the bar, his face mottled with anger.

"The money's gone. All of it!" he raged, shaking his fist at the ceiling. "And we all know who took it."

Knowing full well who Acres referred to, Cody glanced at Hank, expecting him to come to Leighanna's defense. But Hank kept his gaze on the table, his back slumped against the chair, stubbornly refusing to meet Cody's gaze. With a scowl at his friend, Cody pushed to his feet. "Now, Acres," he said, trying to keep a tight rein on his anger. "We don't know for a fact that Leighanna took the money."

The mayor whirled on him. "Then who in the hell do you think did? She was the last one in the office, and it was her job to lock it up in the safe."

"Leighanna didn't steal your money."

Every head turned to stare at Hank. Heat burned his cheeks as he saw the looks of pity that some of the folks turned his way. He didn't want their pity, he'd been pitied enough in his lifetime, a result of his mother's whoring ways. He may have made a mistake in trusting his heart to Leighanna, and he might be humiliated that all his friends were witness to her abandonment of him, but he couldn't remain quiet while they crucified her. She might be a lot of things, but he knew she was no damn thief. "She left me a note," he said gruffly. "Said she'd made a mistake in coming here to Temptation and was going back to Houston. A woman on the run sure as hell wouldn't have told anyone where she was going, not if she had anything to hide."

Cody heaved a sigh of relief, thankful that Hank had at last stood up for Leighanna. He quickly shifted his attention back to the crowd. "There were plenty of strangers in town last night. Any one of them could have broken into that office and stolen the money."

"They must have had the combination, then," Mayor Acres replied dryly. "Because you know as well as I do that that safe had not been tampered with. She probably was working with somebody on the outside."

Cody flattened his hands on the table to keep himself from punching the man in the face. "Did it ever occur to you, or to anybody else in this room," he said with a wave of his hand that encompassed the occupants of the bar, "that Leighanna might very well be the victim here? Did you ever consider the possibility that someone might have *forced* her to give them the money, then kidnapped her, or worse?"

Mary Claire, who was sitting next to Harley, made a strangled sound, then buried her face against Harley's shoulder.

The blood slowly drained from Hank's face. He'd never considered the possibility that Leighanna might be in danger, at least not since he'd found her note. He lifted his head to look at Cody. "There was a man in the trailer with her last night," he said hoarsely, his throat raw from the fear choking him. "A stranger. I'd never seen him before. She seemed a little nervous, and when I asked her if anything was wrong, she said, no, she was fine."

Instantly alert, Cody turned his full attention on Hank. "What did he look like? Can you describe him?"

Hank frowned, trying to remember. "I don't know. Maybe. I'd guess him to be about five foot nine, or so, medium build, dark complexion." His frown deepened as the image grew. "Brown hair, kind of curly and combed straight back," he said, raking his fingers through his own hair to demonstrate. "He—"

Mary Claire lifted her head from Harley's shoulder to stare at Hank, her tear-filled eyes going round. "Roger," she murmured weakly.

Cody whirled. "Who?"

Mary Claire swallowed hard, shifting her gaze from Hank's face to Cody's. "Roger. Leighanna's ex-husband."

Hank felt his heart fall to land in his stomach like a lead ball. Her ex-husband. He remembered the man saying something about them getting together again before he left town. She'd probably gone back to him and hadn't had the nerve to tell Hank of her plans.

Cody's forehead plowed into a frown. "Would he..."

"I don't know," Mary Claire murmured, pressing her fingers to her throbbing temples. "But I do know this," she added emphatically, making her hands into a white-knuckled fist on the table. "Leighanna would never willingly help him."

Cody turned to look at Hank. "Have you checked your safe, yet, to see if anything's missing?"

"I made my deposit yesterday," he said with a dismissive wave of his hand. "There's nothing there but the register drawer and a little start-up cash."

"Wouldn't hurt to check."

Though the thought of Leighanna stealing from him

was a hard concept for Hank to swallow, he did as Cody instructed. He ducked beneath the bar to his safe and turned the dial, listening as the tumblers fell into place. Holding his breath, he wrenched the door open then sagged in relief when he saw the cash drawer lying on the shelf just as he'd left it. But as he started to rise, something else caught his eye. A bank bag lay on the bottom shelf...the same bank bag he'd seen Leighanna shove into the mayor's safe the night before.

His hand shaking, he drew it out, strengthening his grip on it as he took its full weight. Rising, he heaved it onto the bar, narrowing his eyes at the pompous mayor. "There's your money, Acres. I told you Leighanna was no damn thief."

With the mystery of the missing money resolved, there was no reason for anyone to stick around. Folks drifted out of The End of the Road, somewhat subdued, and headed for church or their respective homes. Only Mary Claire, Harley and Cody remained behind.

Silence hung over the foursome as they sat at a table, each consumed by the question that still remained unanswered. It was Mary Claire who finally found the courage to broach the subject of Leighanna's disappearance.

She reached over and covered Hank's hand with hers. "She loves you, Hank. I know she does. She would never purposefully hurt you."

Scowling, Hank pulled his hand from beneath hers, not wanting her pity. "She has a damn funny way of showing it."

Mary Claire shook her head. "I know this all must seem strange to you, but I think I understand why she did what she did."

Hank snorted. "Enlighten me. I'm still in the dark."

Mary Claire drew in a deep breath, wanting desperately for him to understand. "It all revolves around Roger. Knowing him as she does, Leighanna was probably worried that he might try something. By bringing the money here and putting it in your safe instead of leaving it at the office, I think she was trying to protect it."

When Hank continued to stare at her, his face an unreadable mask, she heaved a sigh before going on. "As to why she disappeared, I think that has to do with Roger, too. When she moved here from Houston, she hoped to escape him and the power he held over her. I'm certain that she felt responsible for his coming here and feared that if she stayed, he might, too, and she knew that it wouldn't be long before he'd figure out some new scam to run."

She lifted her hands in a helpless shrug. "In her mind, if she wasn't here, then there would be no reason for him to hang around." She looked at Hank imploringly. "Her sole reason was to protect, not to harm." Once again she leaned to cover his hand with hers. "If you'd call her and talk to her, I'm sure that—"

Hank pushed to his feet, jerking his hand from beneath hers. "Nice try, Mary Claire," he muttered, then turned his back on them all and headed for his apartment. "But no cigar."

Unaware of the fact that her name was on the lips of every person within a fifty-mile radius of Temptation, Leighanna sat on Reggie's sofa, her knees pulled to her chin.

"I don't understand how he found me," she sobbed. "No one but you knew where I went when I left Houston."

Reggie laid a hand on Leighanna's back and rubbed in an effort to comfort. "Knowing Roger, he'd find a way.

I wouldn't put anything past him.'' She continued to rub, her forehead pleating in a frown. ''What I don't understand is why you left Temptation. Mary Claire told me you were head-over-heels for some bartender.''

Leighanna hiccuped and dragged a hand beneath her nose as her thoughts drifted to Hank. Fresh tears flooded her eyes as she realized that by now he would have read the note she had left him. ''I am,'' she said miserably. ''But how could I stay after Roger said what he did, about how the town was ripe for picking?'' She lifted her head, turning her watery gaze on Reggie. ''I would never be able to forgive myself if he took advantage of them in some way. They're good people, Reggie, and they're my friends. I couldn't just stand by and let Roger harm them when I could do something to prevent it.''

Reggie heaved a frustrated breath. ''You aren't responsible for Roger's actions, Leighanna.''

''But I am,'' she cried. ''If I hadn't been in Temptation, he would never have gone there.''

''So what are you going to do, spend your whole life running? You have got to quit protecting him.''

Horrified at the suggestion, Leighanna twisted around to stare at Reggie. ''I'm not protecting him!''

''Sure you are.''

''I am not!''

Reggie heaved a sigh. ''Did you leave Temptation?''

''Yes.''

''Did you leave to keep Roger from doing something stupid?''

Leighanna rubbed at her temples, trying to ease the ache there. ''Well, yes, I suppose.''

''Then you're protecting him. Let him do what he will and suffer the consequences alone.'' She cupped her hand beneath Leighanna's chin, tipping up her face. ''Don't let him rob you of your happiness. Go back to Temptation and to Hank. Go back home.''

Before Leighanna could argue the merits of Reggie's suggestion of returning to Temptation, the phone rang.

Reggie answered it, then held out the phone, cocking one brow at Leighanna. ''It's Mary Claire,'' she said, her voice holding a gentle note of warning.

Leighanna's heart leapt to her throat. *Mary Claire?* If Mary Claire knew to call her at Reggie's, then she must have talked to Hank. He was the only one who knew of her departure for Houston.

''Hello?'' she said, her voice quavering in uncertainty.

Reggie watched Leighanna's eyes widen in shock.

''Leighanna, what is it?'' Reggie whispered in concern. Leighanna waved at the phone and Reggie quickly punched the speaker button so that she could hear the conversation, as well. They both listened, staring at each other in stunned silence while Mary Claire told them of the missing money and the mayor's assumption that Leighanna had stolen it.

''But I didn't take the money!'' she cried, horrified that Mary Claire would think she'd do such a thing.

''I know you didn't,'' Mary Claire consoled her. ''We all know,'' she said, then quickly added, ''at least we do now. We were all gathered at The End of the Road this morning when Hank found the money in his safe.''

Leighanna's eyes, if possible, widened even more. ''All? You mean everyone in town thought I'd stolen the money?''

''Well,'' Mary Claire replied hesitantly, ''you know how Mayor Acres is. He went off the deep end when he discovered it missing and called a town meeting. That's when he accused you of taking it.''

Leighanna pressed a hand to her forehead. ''Oh, my

God,'' she murmured, humiliated to think that everyone in town was privy to her disgrace.

"Don't worry, though," Mary Claire reassured her. "Cody came to your defense."

Leighanna wilted a little more. Not Hank, but Cody. That knowledge hurt more than anything she'd heard thus far.

"Cody refused to believe the mayor's theory," Mary Claire continued, "and was convinced that someone had forced you to give them the money, then kidnapped you, or worse. That's when Hank mentioned seeing a man in the trailer with you the night before. When he described him, I knew the man had to be Roger."

Leighanna's mind whirled with the possibilities that that news offered to her already damned character. "So then, naturally, everyone thought that Roger and I had planned this all along and that we had stolen the money, then escaped," she interjected miserably.

"Not for long. Cody had Hank check his own safe to see if anything was missing, and that's when Hank found the money bag from the festival."

Leighanna's eyes closed at the mention again of Hank's name. "Is he angry with me for leaving?"

She heard Mary Claire's sigh. "Angry or disappointed, I'm not sure. Why don't you call him, Leighanna, explain everything to him? I'm sure he'll understand."

Leighanna shook her head, at first unable to find the strength to utter a refusal. The fact that Hank had failed to defend her hurt more than she was ready to admit. "Maybe later. Not now." Before Mary Claire could argue, she quickly brought the conversation to an end. "Thanks for calling, Mary Claire. And I'm sorry for this whole mess." She quickly replaced the receiver, cutting the connection.

* * *

Mary Claire hung up the phone, her lips pursed in a frustrated frown. She glanced at Harley. "She's not going to call him."

Harley just shook his head. "There's nothing more you can do."

Mary Claire clasped her hands in a fist at her waist and paced away from the phone. "There has to be something. They need each other." She turned to face Harley. "You saw Hank. He was hurting, I just know he was. And Leighanna," she added, tossing up her hands. "She sounded as miserable as Hank looks."

"Now, Mary Claire," Harley soothed. "You've done all you can do."

Mary Claire turned her gaze to the window, her gaze narrowing in contemplation. "There has to be some way we can get them together again."

Working through a blind rage, Hank jerked Leighanna's clothes from the hangers in the closet, her lingerie from the top dresser drawer and stuffed it all into the single suitcase she'd brought with her when she'd moved in. Grabbing a sack from the kitchen, he raked all her toiletries from the bathroom counter, twisted the sack's neck as he'd like to twist her lying neck, then tossed it, too, into the suitcase before slamming it closed.

He marched angrily for the shed out back, ripped open the door, tossed the suitcase inside, then slammed the door on the unwanted reminder. Returning to his apartment, he caught a glimpse of the geraniums blooming on the windowsill and with a growl, jerked open the window and gave the pots an angry shove. He listened to the sound of the clay pots shattering on the ground below and felt the same fissures splintering his heart. Bracing his hands on the windowsill, he dipped his head, his shoulders heaving, his anger slowly giving way to misery.

He loved her. Even though he'd never found the courage to tell her, he loved her. And now she was gone.

Heaving himself away from the window, he strode for the door and the outside. The geraniums lay amongst the shards of broken pottery and clumps of dirt. Carefully, he picked the plants up, dusting the soil from the blooms and carried them back inside.

"Have you talked to Leighanna?" Cody asked.

Hank stuck a mug beneath the spigot and filled it with beer. "No. Was I supposed to?" he asked sourly as he shoved the mug Cody's way.

Cody glanced at Harley who sat on the stool beside him then shrugged. "No. Just thought you might have called her."

Hank filled another mug and plopped it down in front of Harley. "And why would I do that?"

"I don't know. Just thought you might be curious to know why she up and left so unexpectedly. She seemed happy enough while she was here."

Hank bit back a frown. He'd wondered all right, but his pride wouldn't allow him to admit that to his friends.

Harley lifted his mug and took a sip, eyeing Hank over its rim. "Mary Claire talked to her," he said quietly.

Hank snapped his head up to look at Harley, then quickly turned away, refusing to ask the questions that burned in his mind.

Cody didn't feel the same compunction. "Where is she?"

"In Houston," Harley replied. "She's staying with a friend."

"Is she planning on coming back to Temptation?" Cody asked.

Harley watched Hank's shoulders stiffen reflexively and said, "Didn't say, though I've wondered about that. Not more than a day or two before she left, she talked to Mary Claire about leasing her house after we get married. Seemed real excited at the prospect, too."

Hank had heard about all he could stand. He wheeled back around to glare at his two friends. "If you two came here to try to pressure me into calling Leighanna, you can haul your asses right back out, because I'm not going to. *She's* the one who left. *She's* the one who'll have to call me. Hank Braden crawls to no woman!"

"Damn nosey busybodies," Hank muttered as he carefully poured water over the geraniums he'd replanted. "Coming over here, thinking they can coerce me into calling Leighanna. Humph," he snorted, and tossed the plastic watering can into the sink. "They're wasting their time."

Opening the refrigerator, he pulled out a beer, then grabbed the plate with the sandwich he'd made. Heading for the bed, he stretched out, balancing the plate on his stomach. He refused to eat at the table where he'd shared his meals with Leighanna, reverting instead to his old habit of eating in bed. He knew it was a childish act of defiance, especially since Leighanna wasn't even there to witness his rebellion, but it made him feel a little better knowing he was doing something she wouldn't approve of.

Just thought you might be curious to know why she up and left so unexpectedly. She seemed happy enough while she was here. Cody's comment came out of nowhere and settled itself in Hank's mind.

Yeah, he'd wondered all right. Had spent hours, lying awake in his bed at night, weighing all the possibilities.

Not more than a day or two before she left, she talked

to Mary Claire about leasing her house after we get married. Seemed real excited at the prospect, too.

Hank's grip on his sandwich slackened and it slipped from his fingers and fell back to the plate as Harley's words wormed their way into his conscience to replace Cody's. He remembered well the afternoon that she'd approached him about the two of them leasing Mary Claire's house...and remembered, too, her disappointment when he'd refused to consider her suggestion.

Was that why she'd left him? he wondered. Was it because she wanted more than he was willing to give?

Fearing that he was the one who was responsible for her leaving, he set aside the plate and sat up.

He wanted to hate her, rail at her for what she'd done to him...but for some reason he couldn't work up the strength required to do even that. Not any more. He missed her. Missed the warmth of her smile, the satisfaction of waking up with her beside him each morning, missed her working alongside him at the bar.

He loved her...but he'd never had the courage to share those feelings with her.

He dug his fingers through his hair, cursing himself for allowing his own fears of commitment to rob him of the only happiness he'd known in his whole sorry life.

Hank set his purchases on the counter and waited while Mrs. Martin rang them up.

"Have you seen or talked to Leighanna since she left?" Mrs. Martin asked as she weighed a sack of tomatoes.

Hank felt heat crawl up his neck as he heard almost the same question Cody had posed to him asked again. "No," he replied, hoping the inquisition would stop there.

Mrs. Martin pulled the sack of tomatoes from the scale

and punched in the price on her cash register. "You're just gonna let her go, then?"

"She's the one who left," Hank reminded her.

"Humph," was Mrs. Martin's reply. She picked up a frozen TV dinner and frowned at it. "I'd imagine that it would be hard for her to make the first move, considering all that happened."

Hank's forehead plowed into a frown, unable to follow her line of thought. "And why's that?"

Mrs. Martin punched in a couple more items and dropped them in a sack before lifting her shoulder in a shrug. "What with all Mayor Acres's ravings, accusing her of being a thief, I'm sure she'd just as soon forget she ever set foot in this town." She glanced at Hank over the top of her smudged glasses and gave him a knowing look. "Can't say as I blame her, either, with everybody ready to hang her, and her being innocent and all."

When he didn't reply, she merely lifted her shoulder in a shrug again and pushed his sack of purchases toward him. "I suppose you'll be going to Harley and Mary Claire's engagement party Sunday night?"

He picked up his sack. "Plan on it."

"Wonder if Leighanna will show up?" Mrs. Martin mused, eyeing him curiously. "A person would think she might, since she's one of Mary Claire's best friends."

Hank turned for the door without answering, his thoughts spinning crazily. He'd never considered the possibility of Leighanna returning for the party.

Would she come? he wondered. And what would he do if she did? What could he say to make up for ever doubting her? For not having had the courage to tell her he loved her? For not immediately following her and begging her to return?

A thought began to take shape in his mind, and he pushed through the door, dumped the sack of groceries in the back of his truck and headed for the hardware store across the street.

Reggie tossed the invitation onto Leighanna's lap and strode for the kitchen. "As much as I hate to miss it, I can't go."

Leighanna picked up the invitation she'd just handed to Reggie and stared in dismay at her retreating back. "But one of us has to go!" she cried. "Mary Claire's our friend."

Reggie's reply was muffled by the refrigerator door. "Then you go. I'm sorry, but I've got to work."

Leighanna dipped her head, staring blindly at the invitation. "I can't," she murmured miserably, knowing that if she went she was bound to see Hank. She didn't think she could bear it if he shunned her. "At least not yet."

Reggie appeared in the kitchen doorway, cradling a bottle of mineral water in one hand. "And waiting is going to make seeing him any easier?"

Ten

By Sunday morning Leighanna was a wreck, torn by her obligation to Mary Claire and her reluctance to confront Hank and all the other people of Temptation again.

I'm a coward, she told herself as she paced furiously around Reggie's guest room. Nothing but a sniveling little coward. Mary Claire is my best friend. How can I possibly let her down on such a special occasion such as this?

I won't! she told herself defiantly. She stripped her borrowed nightgown over her head and tossed it to the floor. She hadn't done anything wrong. She had nothing to be ashamed of. She'd wanted only to protect the people of Temptation, including Hank, and if they wanted to condemn her for that, well let them!

Besides, she told herself, as she jerked on some clothes. She missed Hank. She loved him, for heaven's sake! And if she had to fight for him as Mary Claire had once suggested, then she was prepared to duke it out with whomever necessary, even Hank if that's what it took to knock some sense in his head. He loved her, she knew he did, and she wouldn't let him get by without admitting it. Not this time.

She stopped in front of the dresser mirror, narrowing her eyes at her reflection as she drew her right hand into a fist and pounded it into her left. After all, she told herself, I have a pretty mean right hook. Hank had said so himself.

Hank knelt in front of the freshly planted shrubs in front of The End of the Road, frantically nailing pickets into place. He paused long enough in his work to wipe the sweat from his brow and glance at his wristwatch. Just past five and the party started at six. He twisted his head around to look at the road behind him where the sun created a hazy mirage on the hot asphalt. He knew that if she was coming, she had to pass by this way, as this was the only road that led to Harley's from Temptation.

He frowned, shoving back the doubts that suddenly crowded his mind. She'd be there, he told himself and picked up his hammer again. Leighanna was too good a person to let Mary Claire down.

But would she come by to see him? Would she stop when she saw what he'd done? Would she even bother to glance this way? He tightened his fingers on the hammer. Didn't matter whether she noticed or not, he told himself as he slammed another nail into the picket he held, because he was going to that party and if she was there, he was going to talk to her and insist that she come home to The End of the Road where she—

Before he could even finish the thought, he heard a car on the highway in the distance and knew without even turning it was Leighanna. He'd recognize that clanking engine anywhere. He held his breath as the sound of the car drew nearer and thought sure his lungs were going to burst wide open when he heard the car slow. Twisting at the waist, he turned and saw that she'd stopped right smack-dab in the middle of the highway at the entrance to the bar's parking lot.

With his heart in his throat, willing her to come to him, needing that sign that she still cared, he stood and waited. It seemed an eternity passed before she made the turn, swinging her car onto the gravel lot...and Hank finally breathed his first full breath that day.

She braked to a gravel-spitting stop in front of him and climbed out, that dang door of hers screeching on its unoiled hinges, sending a shiver down his spine, before she slammed it shut. He watched her stomp toward him and slowly became aware of the stiffness in her shoulders, in the determined, angry slant of her mouth.

She stopped in front of him, her chin cocked high as she glared at him through narrowed eyes. "You know what, Braden?" she ground out. "You always took pleasure in calling me a coward. Me!" she repeated, her voice rising an octave. "When you're the one who's the coward!" She lifted a hand to poke a stiff finger at his chest. "*You're* the one who's afraid. Afraid to share your feelings for fear you'll get hurt. Afraid to commit yourself to something that has no guarantees. Well, I'm not afraid," she raged on. "I love you. I told you that before and my feelings haven't changed. I'm—"

"I love you, too."

"—not afraid to admit that. I—" She suddenly stopped as what he'd said soaked through the red haze of her anger. Her mouth went round in a silent "oh" and she fell back a step. "What did you say?"

Smiling, Hank took a step toward her, closing the dis-

tance she'd put between them. "I said, I love you." He
cupped his hand along the line of her jaw, tipping her
face to his. "And you know what? Saying it isn't nearly
as scary as the thought of losing you."

She sucked in a breath, not trusting her ears. "But I
thought..."

"That I didn't love you? That I'd let you go without
putting up a fight?" he asked softly.

Leighanna closed her eyes and turned away from his
hand, her mind whirling in confusion. She was the one
who was supposed to be fighting for him. Hadn't she
made that decision that very morning while staring at her
own reflection in Reggie's mirror? With the tables reversed on her, she didn't know what to say, what to do.

She opened her eyes...and saw for the first time the
newly planted shrubs...and the fence. Her hand went instinctively to cover her heart. When she lifted her face
to look at Hank, there were tears on her cheeks...and
Hank was sure that his heart was going to split right in
two.

He took a step toward her, then stopped, unsure of
what to say.

She looked at him, her eyes filled with questions.
"You planted the shrubs," she murmured.

He lifted a shoulder in a shrug. "You said it was what
the bar needed."

She swallowed hard, turning her gaze to the newly
erected fence, wondering what all this meant and afraid
to put more meaning behind its appearance than Hank
had intended.

Hank saw the direction of her gaze and took another
step closer. "I know the fence isn't exactly what you had
in mind, but it was the best I could do at the moment."

Her mouth opened as if she was about to say something, then closed again. She pressed trembling fingers to

her lips, and new tears came to chase those that already dampened her cheeks. This time Hank couldn't keep himself for reaching out to her. She fell into his arms on a strangled sob.

"Oh, Leighanna, baby," he murmured, holding her close. "Please don't cry." He rocked her in his arms, burying his nose in her hair, glorying in the feel of her again in his arms after so many days without her. "I'm sorry I didn't come after you. I know that I should have, that I shouldn't have let pride stand in my way." He pushed her to arm's length, needing to see her face, his heart nearly breaking all over again at the pain he saw there when he knew he was the cause. "Tell me you'll forgive me?"

Leighanna looked up at him through watery eyes and shook her head. "N-no," she stammered, scraping the tears from beneath her eyes. "You don't have anything to be sorry about. I should never have left." Fresh tears swelled as she closed her hands over the arms that held her. "I didn't want to leave you. I swear I didn't. I just wanted to protect everyone from Roger."

"I know, I know," he soothed. "Mary Claire told me the same damn thing, only I couldn't see beyond the hurt to believe it. Oh, God, Leighanna," he said, crushing her to him. "I've missed you so much."

Laughing through her tears, she threw her arms around his neck and clung. "And I missed you, Hank. More than you'll ever know."

They stood, the sun shining warm on their backs, their hearts thundering against each other. It was Hank who finally pulled away. He took a step back and dipped his head down, suffering a sudden attack of nerves and unable to meet her gaze. "Leighanna," he said, nervously digging the toe of his boot into the gravel. "I have a confession to make."

Her eyes grew round, and her heart stuttered to a stop. "A confession? What kind of confession?"

"I've been eating in bed again."

Expecting something much worse, like maybe Betty Jo had been back in town, Leighanna nearly collapsed in relief. "Shame on you," she chided, unable to keep from laughing.

He looked up at the sound of her laughter and grinned. He reached out and caught her hand in his, lacing his fingers through hers, and the grin slowly melted. "I just couldn't bring myself to sit at that table without you there with me."

Emotion rose to Leighanna's throat. "Oh, Hank..."

"I did water your geraniums, though I think they've lost a few blooms." His fingers tightened on hers. "We need you, Leighanna. Me and those dumb geraniums. We're liable to just wilt and die without you here to care for us."

"Oh, Hank..." she said again, fighting back tears.

"I love you, Leighanna. I want you to move back in, I—"

"Yes," she cried before he could finish. "I—"

He squeezed her hand, silencing her. "Let me finish. I want you to move back in, all right, but I want you to move back in as my wife."

Leighanna's eyes grew round, her mouth dropping open. "Your wife?" she gasped out on a hoarse whisper.

Hank frowned. "I know I'm not much of a catch, and I'm barely housebroke by most women's standards, but I promise that I'll give you all your dreams. We'll start with that house you've always wanted, the one with the white picket—"

Before he could say more, Leighanna was in his arms, her hands cinched tight around his neck. "Oh, Hank," she sobbed. "I don't need a house, or a picket fence. All I need is you."

And all of him was exactly what Hank was prepared to give.

*   *   *   *   *

ATTENTION
ALL JOAN JOHNSTON FANS!

Silhouette Books is pleased to bring you two brand-new
additions to the #1 bestselling Hawk's Way series—the
novel you've all been waiting for and a short story....

*"Joan Johnston does contemporary westerns to
perfection."* —*Publishers Weekly*

**Remember those Whitelaws of Texas
from Joan Johnston's HAWK'S WAY
series? Jewel Whitelaw is all grown up and is
about to introduce Mac Macready to the wonders
of passion! You see, Mac is a virgin...and it's going
to be one long, hot summer....**

HAWK'S WAY
THE VIRGIN GROOM
August 1997

And in November don't miss Rolleen Whitelaw's
love story, *A HAWK'S WAY CHRISTMAS*, in
LONE STAR CHRISTMAS, a fabulous new
holiday keepsake collection by talented authors
Joan Johnston and Diana Palmer. Their heroes are
seductive, shameless and irresistible—and these
Texans are experts in sneaking kisses under the
mistletoe! So get ready for a sizzling holiday season....

Only from ▼ *Silhouette*®

Take 4 bestselling love stories FREE

Plus get a FREE surprise gift!

Special Limited-time Offer

Mail to Silhouette Reader Service™

3010 Walden Avenue
P.O. Box 1867
Buffalo, N.Y. 14240-1867

YES! Please send me 4 free Silhouette Desire® novels and my free surprise gift. Then send me 6 brand-new novels every month, which I will receive months before they appear in bookstores. Bill me at the low price of $2.90 each plus 25¢ delivery and applicable sales tax, if any.* That's the complete price and a savings of over 10% off the cover prices—quite a bargain! I understand that accepting the books and gift places me under no obligation ever to buy any books. I can always return a shipment and cancel at any time. Even if I never buy another book from Silhouette, the 4 free books and the surprise gift are mine to keep forever.

225 BPA A3UU

Name	(PLEASE PRINT)	
Address	Apt. No.	
City	State	Zip

This offer is limited to one order per household and not valid to present *Silhouette Desire®* subscribers. *Terms and prices are subject to change without notice.
Sales tax applicable in N.Y.

UDES-696 ©1990 Harlequin Enterprises Limited

They called her the

Champagne Girl

Catherine: Underneath the effervescent, carefree and bubbly
facade there was a depth to which few
had access.

Matt: The older stepbrother she inherited with her
mother's second marriage, Matt continually
complicated things. It seemed to Catherine that
she would make plans only to have Matt foul
them up.

With the perfect job waiting in New York City, only one thing
would be able to keep her on a dusty cattle ranch: something
she thought she could never have—the love of the sexiest
cowboy in the Lone Star state.

by bestselling author

DIANA PALMER

Available in September 1997 at your favorite retail outlet.

MIRA **The brightest star in women's fiction**   MDP8

Look us up on-line at: http://www.romance.net

FANTASTIC NEWS!

For all you devoted Diana Palmer fans
Silhouette Books is pleased to bring you
a brand-new novel and short story by one of the
top ten romance writers in America

"Nobody tops Diana Palmer...I love her stories."
—*New York Times* bestselling author
Jayne Ann Krentz

Diana Palmer has written another thrilling desire.
Man of the Month Ramon Cortero was a talented
surgeon, existing only for his work—until the
night he saved nurse Noreen Kensington's life. But
their stormy past makes this romance a challenge!

THE PATIENT NURSE
Silhouette Desire
October 1997

And in November Diana Palmer adds to the
Long, Tall Texans series with *CHRISTMAS COWBOY*, in
LONE STAR CHRISTMAS, a fabulous new holiday
keepsake collection by talented authors Diana Palmer
and Joan Johnston. Their heroes are seductive,
shameless and irresistible—and these Texans are
experts at sneaking kisses under the mistletoe! So get
ready for a sizzling holiday season....

Only from ▼ *Silhouette*®